MEGGIE'S JOURNEYS

MEGGIE'S JOURNEYS

by

MARGARET D'AMBROSIO

POLYGON
Edinburgh

First published in Great Britain in 1987 by
Polygon, 48 Pleasance,
Edinburgh EH8 9TJ.

Typeset 11/13 point Erhardt by
EUSPB, 48 Pleasance,
Edinburgh EH8 9TJ.

Printed by Bell & Bain Ltd.,
Glasgow.

ISBN 0 948275 44 8

Cover design by Tim Robertson.
Cover illustration by Hazel McGlashan.

To the Old Ones:
nothing is ever forgotten.

ACKNOWLEDGEMENTS

THE poem by A. W. E. O'Shaughnessy was gleaned from the title page of *The Music Makers* by E. V. Thompson.

The verses from *Tamlane* are from *The English and Scottish Popular Ballads*, vol. 1, ed. Francis James Child, Dover Publications, New York. They are from Ballad 39, versions I and F.

AUTHOR'S NOTE

THE Otherworld of the Celts was not remote like the Christian Heaven. It co-existed with nature in earth, sky and sea as a parallel reality, perceived through the inner senses and the visionary, intuitive part of the mind. It was divided primarily into four realms, each with its own distinct characteristics and inhabitants, corresponding to the four elements of Earth, Air, Fire and Water. These four elements, in varying proportions, were held by the ancients to be the underlying constituents of every natural creation, including man.

At times and places of transition, such as dusk, dawn, the shore of the sea, sacred sites, doorways and bridges, the barrier of consciousness which separated the Otherworld from everyday reality was thin, and could more easily be crossed. Perhaps the most potent times of transition were the four great quarter-day festivals which divided the Celtic year into seasons, and it is on those days that Meggie undertook her journeys into the realms of the Otherworld. They are as follows:

Samhain (pronounced 'sou-in') — October 31st-November 1st — corresponding to the modern Hallowe'en, was the Feast of the Dead. It was the start of the Celtic New Year and the season of Winter, and was associated with the direction North, the element of Earth, and the life-phase of Death and Rebirth.

Imbolc — January 31st-February 1st — corresponding to the modern Candlemas, was the Feast of Lights, celebrating the coming to life of nature in Spring. It was also associated with the direction East, the element of Air and the life-phase of Youth.

Beltane — April 30th-May 1st — corresponding to the modern May Day, was the Feast of the Sun which heralded Summer. It was associated with the direction South, the element of Fire and the life-phase of Maturity.

Lughnasadh (pronounced 'loohh-na-sa') — July 31st-August 1st — corresponding to the modern Lammas, was the Feast of Corn, also associated with the direction West, the element of Water and the life-phase of Old Age.

The Sidhe (pronounced 'shee'), whom Meggie meets on her first four journeys into the Otherworld, were a tall, noble, fair-featured race of spiritual beings who were associated with ancestors and mythical heroes, as well as with elementals, nature spirits and faeries. They were said to inhabit many of the wild and hauntingly beautiful places of the Celtic landscape, and there are many recorded sightings of them and journeys into their realms. They were not, generally speaking, inimical, and often gave generously of their powers of artistry and magic to help human evolution, but close contact with them had a way of exacting its own price.

Meggie's fifth journey is into the element of Ether: the Mystical Centre of Celtic cosmology from which the other four elements of creation spring, corresponding to the direction 'Here'. It is the quintessential Soul of Nature that gives life to the universe, and purifies human consciousness.

The sixth and final journey is one of completion, integration and unity, where beginnings and endings are one and the same. This corresponds to the Druidic Plane of the Sun, while Ether is the Plane of the Moon, and the first four elements together comprise the Plane of the Earth.

MEGGIE'S JOURNEYS

We are the music-makers,
And we are the dreamers of dreams
Wandering by lone sea-breakers,
And sitting by desolate streams;
World-losers and world-forsaken,
On whom the pale Moon gleams:
Yet we are the movers and shakers
Of the world for ever, it seems.

A. W. E. O'Shaughnessy

Part One

The Hollow Hill

Chapter 1

SAMHAIN MISTS

IT was the eve of Samhain. The winter sun shimmering pale upon the far horizon across the sea surrendered without struggle to the dark-fingered night clouds. The long shadows of dusk growing imperceptibly upon the curves of the land, patterning it in light and shade, silently told of the time that was no time: neither night nor day, neither old year nor new, neither death nor life. It was that secret hour of wonders and of fear when each faced their own truth unveiled; when past, present and future merged into the unity that they are within a dream.

Poised upon the brink of that dream, her thoughts no longer truly her own as they absorbed the resonance of the twilight, stood Meggie alone at the cottage door. Quite still she stood for a while, adjusting to the shifting tides, affirming her balance in the centre of the Four Elements of Fire, Air, Water and Earth. As tokens, she held in her right hand a pinewood torch, which scented the air with resin-smoke as it burned, and in her left, a bowl of salted spring water. Flame for Fire, pine-scent for Air, salt for Earth mingled with the Water of life — symbols as old as time itself, powerful and pure. When at last it felt right, she began to walk slowly round the little house, circling it as the sun does and blessing it with the Elements as she went.

Samhain eve was an unchancy time when the delicate tissue of life that Nature wove throughout the year was threatened by the archaic rumblings of chaos. But there was no real danger, Meggie knew, as long as each who could undertook to uphold some threads of that tissue intact on behalf of the whole, to help maintain the natural order until time breathed again and life continued as it should. She circled the house in ritual balance with the Elements to protect herself, her family and homestead, to preserve the serenity of the gentle glens above the white-shelled beach where she belonged, and to ensure the continuity of the way of life that felt right to her.

However, it seemed as she circled for the third time that, just as the colours of the landscape merged into the purply darkness of the night, so she was becoming tinged with an awareness of being different to her own, beyond the span of the sun and life as she knew it. She struggled a little with the unfamiliar feeling, then realised that fear was her only enemy in the face of the unknown. With a deep sigh she released her fear, and, as it dispersed into the thick night air, it began to dawn on her that her life was no longer in her own hands.

Then, as if in echo, the flame of the pine-torch guttered and died.

* * *

Afterwards, she could never be sure whether the cloaked figure had walked down the steep slopes beyond, or simply materialised before her from the fabric of the night mists. She knew only that she had heard neither footfall nor hoof-beat, nor seen any traveller's lamp approaching through the darkness, and yet she was somehow aware that the stranger had come from the far north, beyond the hills and gullies that Meggie could name. It was not often that people came by the land route from the north, for it felt treacherous and bitter even in the gentle sun of summer. It was more usual to travel by boat, for the little sheltered cove to the south-west made a perfect natural harbour.

But, however unusual it was, a stranger was a stranger and, even on an uncanny night like this, deserved hospitality.

"The blessings of the Elements upon you," said Meggie in traditional greeting.

"May Sun and Moon light your path," replied the stranger gently.

It was not the usual reply, but then maybe things were different in the north country. However, at least from this answer Meggie could be sure that this was no entity sent to suck her life-blood into the whirlwinds of chaos. She sensed suddenly that the stranger had caught her suspicion, and faltered with embarrassment.

"Forgive me, but it is the unknown hour of the year's change. I was unsure who you might be . . ."

The stranger stopped her with an unexpected tinkle of laughter. "You did right to doubt, my child, for caution was ever the handmaiden of wisdom. No harm is done, for I have nothing to hide."

"Then what do they call you?" asked Meggie with a sudden boldness.

"Through the long ages I have been known by many names, but you may call me Annis."

This again was not the usual answer. It seemed clear amidst uncertainty that this was no ordinary person. Meggie was unsure what to do next and simply stared. At that the figure removed the hood of her cloak to reveal an old woman's face, as lined and craggy as treebark, yet with eyes that were as limpid and open as those of a young fawn who has never known fear. This was someone to be trusted as you could trust the animals and trees; someone who knew life's secrets without being told.

"Come," said the old one.

She stretched out her hand, and, as Meggie reached out to grasp it, she moved from the familiar sight of her little white house on the hillside into the unformed swirl of the Samhain mists.

Chapter 2

HUNT AND MAZE

WHEN the mists cleared at last, she saw two white horses before her, tethered to an ancient oak on the edge of a dark, unfamiliar forest. They were richly caparisoned in green cloths and red leather reins with tiny bells that sounded as the horses tossed their heads. Never before had Meggie seen such magnificent creatures, so different from the shaggy brown ponies that pulled carts in her own glens. She was thrilled when Annis untied them and helped her to mount one. Upon its back she felt like a queen.

"Ragwort is his name," said Annis. "Tell him to fly like the wind to his home."

"Ragwort, up and away!" shouted Meggie with a command she never knew she possessed. Immediately, the great beast soared high and fast into the sky, with Annis on the other horse close behind. The roaring of the wind in her ears seemed like the galloping of many hooves, and out of the corner of her eye she saw a great host of white horses around and behind her, all ridden by small figures dressed in green. Looking down at herself, she saw that she was now clad in a gown of green velvet with long red ribbons that streamed out into the night. Faster and faster they flew upon the wind as if on some secret chase, and Meggie whooped in delight with the wild freedom that surged through her as the pace quickened.

She was never to forget that feeling, and often returned to the hunt in her dreams, but at last in that other time it was over, so that when she looked round again there were only Annis and herself riding through the woodland. She wondered then if the other white horses she thought she had seen were merely glimmers of moonlight flashing through the trees as they passed, but there was no way of knowing for sure.

They came at last to a wide clearing in the forest, lit by the canopy of stars. The horses slowed down to circle a grassy knowe at its centre and eventually came to a halt. Annis and Meggie dismounted and climbed up to a dark furrow near the top of the little knowe. As they neared it, it curiously seemed to heighten, so that when they set foot upon its shadow it was as tall as they and curved over their heads like a cave. Then, as they walked on into it, it seemed to deepen slightly before their steps so that they never quite reached its end. By the time Meggie was really aware of what was happening, they were deep inside the knowe itself, with moon and stars nowhere to be seen.

* * *

The narrow tunnel was dimly lit by a faint green glimmer whose vein-like threads seemed to support and to shape the walls and roof. Annis and Meggie could see only a few feet ahead of them at any time, so that it always looked as if the unpredictable twists and curves were forming themselves out of the blackness just as they walked. The way was not difficult to follow, but the path behind them vanished from view as suddenly as it had appeared, so there was nothing to measure their progress by.

On and on they turned, now sharply, now gently, now to left and now to right, until Meggie began to feel in despair that they were travelling in the same twisted circles over and over again. She bit back her protests for a while, but was just on the brink of insisting that they turn back when the passage itself began to straighten out into a series of domed arches, each higher and wider than the one before, and each flanked by thick pillars emitting the same greeny fluorescence that had lit the tunnel.

They stopped at last before a great double door, whose surface was beautifully decorated with loops and whorls of the green light. Meggie thought at first that they were hieroglyphs of some strange language, like the signs of power carved upon the Long Stones of home, but when she inspected them more closely, she saw that the door was of wood, and that the light flowed in its grain-lines, knots and burrs. Of course! The tunnel itself was under the forest, carved out of the earth by the interweaving of the roots of countless trees. So the greeny glow was the living energy of those trees!

Annis, who had remained silent throughout the journey in the tunnel, now turned to Meggie with a smile as she caught her thoughts.

"Well done, my child," she said. "You learn quickly. Now will you enter?"

Meggie pushed and tugged at the great door with all her might, but it would not budge. She looked at Annis, who was smiling calmly, herself now glowing with a faint aura of green.

"Who am I, and who is the tree?" she whispered to Meggie. "Are we not all one within the earth? Look at yourself!"

Meggie looked down at the green gown as soft as leaves, and saw her own arm glowing with the same force. She reached out and touched the door again, this time gently following the curves of the fine green lines with her fingers. It suddenly seemed to her that she knew the twists and turns of the tunnel as if she belonged to it, and had shared in the secrets of its making. She knew she could talk to this door as tree talks to tree, and it would surely understand.

"By oak and ash and thorn," she intoned, "open and let me in."

Silently the great door opened, and Meggie and Annis entered the hall of the Sidhe.

Chapter 3

THE FEASTING HALL

M EGGIE stood dazzled for a while as the impact of the noisy throng and the sheer magnificence of the hall hit her unexpectedly after the cool, green silence of the tunnel. Annis had been greeted immediately on entering with a loud hail of welcome from a thousand beautiful faery beings, and had been swept off into the festive crowds out of sight, but Meggie was glad to have been left unnoticed under the shadow of the great door, to take in her new surroundings gradually.

The hall was circular, and so large that she could barely see to the far end. Instead of straight walls and a roof, it was capped by a high vaulted dome, held in place only by the thin lines of green light that covered it like a web — plant roots, as Meggie now knew. It occurred to her that the tummock that they had entered in the forest clearing must be the outside of the very tip of this dome. If that was indeed so, then the twisting, winding tunnel had led them in a spiral maze all around its outside to the door at the very bottom. It was difficult to estimate how big it was, but she guessed it must have been at least the size of one of the hills to the north of her home which was topped by snow even in midsummer. And all underground!

She reeled momentarily at the thought of the great weight of earth over her head at that moment, but managed to pull herself together before panic overwhelmed. Stout-hearted common sense told her instead to make the best of the situation and to take the opportunity to explore. She tentatively sidled into the shadowy recesses of the hall, where she thought she could still remain unseen if necessary. Once she was properly inside, though, her human caution soon gave way to fascination at the glamourie about her. Meggie was simply entranced by its beauty.

All around the edges of the dome she saw luxuriant clumps of leaves and flowers hanging, constantly growing and changing, and shining like coloured lamps over the feasting tables. These were decked with the most handsome plates of gold, goblets of jewelled silver and exquisitely crafted tools of crystal with which to spoon and cut. Then there were the tablecloths of green linen, which were embroidered down the front panels with intricate coiling patterns that seemed to move as you looked at them, suggesting birds in flight, animals running or children playing. Best of all, though, was the food: glowing and glittering with goodness and abundant beyond belief.

There were fruits and nuts of all kinds — many of which Meggie had never seen before — little bannocks and soft breads of different grains, bowls of cream, fragrant cheeses, rich butter, and the sweet honeys of many herbs. Craggins so fine you could see through them stood filled with the sparkling juices of fruits and the sap of trees, spring water, spiced wines and mead. Exotic vegetables were delicately cut, and arranged enticingly in pictures and sculptures on beds of succulent green leaves. Their colours and aromas were such a rich feast to Meggie's senses that she felt filled and renewed without a drop or crumb even passing her lips. Such was the power of magic there that night.

Fully replenished, and now quite at ease with the strange atmosphere of the underhill hall, her curiosity drew her next towards the soft greeny radiance emanating from its centre. At first she thought it was simply a light, perhaps from a fallen star, but as she approached and her eyes attuned to it, she realised that it came from the Sidhe folk themselves, who were gathered there in great numbers round the thrones of the King and Queen, to participate in the evening's entertainment. Each one was shining with a rare and exquisite joy that words could never capture — though countless legends have tried — and this they expressed through delicate songs, with irresistibly nimble tunes that soon had Meggie's heart leaping in delight along with her limbs in endless, tireless dances.

Samhain was the grandest feast of the Sidhe: their festival of Life, to celebrate the brief time when the dead ones of the earthly world were able to shed their dense bodies of clay, and so feel the quickness of spirit and the yearning in their souls that reunited them with their living kinfolk in the Hollow Hills. Their musical festivities were exuberant thanksgiving for the sheer pleasure of living, loving and being together that they felt for the timeless while that the two worlds met.

But just as chill winter winds can swirl suddenly through summer-green grasses, Meggie began to feel their intense joy infuse with a deep inconsolable sadness. The merry dance tunes became haunting airs, and gave way at last to laments that would melt a heart of stone. They told of the poison arrows of hate and fear with which men from the southern lands were beginning to wound them, and how these incurable wounds drained them of their vitality and sparkle, forcing them to recede evermore into the mists and far places of the earth where the destructive emotions of man could not reach them. They told how they missed the simple earth-folk of old, and of their sorrow in banishment from hearth, home, byre and field. They sung their regret of the passing of the legendary Foretime, when they could freely walk in the lands under the sun amongst the first-born of Earth's children. And they told of times to come, when they would be so unable to withstand the baneful miasma of the thoughts of selfish man that the plants would lose their power to nourish, and the wild things would lie dying by silent, mourning trees, while man himself, embittered and impoverished, his rootless feet aimlessly wandering upon a land to which he no longer belonged and in which he was no longer welcome, would never more find peace.

At last Meggie could stand no more, for her heart was close to breaking with shame at her own kind. She sunk to her knees in pain in front of the throne of the Queen, whose regal splendour somehow now looked terrible and foreboding.

"Stop them singing so!" she pleaded. "I would give my life if I could so that these dreadful things would never happen!" Around her, she heard the Sidhe people gasp and whisper at her words.

"Hush, child," replied the Queen gently, lifting Meggie's face and wiping away the tears with her own fine silken cloth. "Say no more, for words spoken in this place come true by the most uncanny means. But to soften the harm that is already done I will teach you something of our ways, so that you may know that the future each mortal faces has been woven by his own truth, and changes as he changes."

She lifted Meggie close to her, and tenderly laid the girl's head in her own lap, stroking her hair as a mother might do to soothe her child. As she did so, she told of the Sidhe of the Hollow Hills, who fashion the forms of trees and plants in precise harmony, instilling each variety with its own elixir of the secret rays of planets and of stars to give it its healing virtue, colours, fragrance and pattern of growth. She talked of the Shining Ones of the Earth who shape the landscape continually to allow the changing Earth-currents to flow freely, as the aeons of evolution turn. She talked, too, of the little beings who tend all that lives upon the Earth, without whose tireless ministrations Nature would perish. And then she talked of Man for whom they all worked that he might be nourished with the goodness and bounty of the Earth; Man who gave their work meaning through the mediation of his mind. Then she talked of the power of the mind itself, that could be used to wreck as well as to nurture.

All the while she listened, Meggie felt deeply at peace

and, as she looked out from her tear-dimmed eyes, it seemed to her that she could see the things the Queen described forming within the radiant aura of the Sidhe that surrounded her, and hear the sounds of Nature in the music that they played. She saw the changes of the seasons overtake one another in succession from the dawn of time to the far horizons of the future, until at last she felt older than the hills themselves.

The Queen felt her slump and called Annis over. "The day has been long for the little one. Guard her well on her journey home."

Between them, they supported Meggie's tired body up to the great door of the feasting hall. There the Queen bade her farewell, and slung a green woollen bag over her shoulder in which she placed a golden plate wrapped in white linen.

"Guard this plate well," she warned Meggie, "for it has been blessed this night by all the powers of the Earth that I know. Carve upon it the sacred symbols and the virtue will shine forth from it. Then you will know it as a true gift from Queen Olwen Underhill. Go now, for time is moving in the world and the mists are shifting. Fare you well, and blessed be."

Meggie would have replied, but her head was swimming with exhaustion, as if she had aged a hundred years overnight. She let Annis wrap her in a coarse dark travelling cloak and hug her close as they walked together. One painful step, two and three, she counted, but then she faltered, and fell upon the damp earth unable to go on. She looked up to Annis for help, but saw only the moon shining amid the stars in the sky above. In front of her was her own cottage, its white walls glimmering palely in the night light, but with only unwelcoming darkness coming from its little windows. Was she too late then? Had some disaster she could vaguely recall really struck her family? Her mind felt numb, and full of strange twirling pictures that would not settle or clear. Perhaps she had fallen and hit her head upon a rock?

Just then she saw a light coming from a cottage further up the glen — a never-so-welcome sight. Perhaps, she thought, whoever lived there could tell her what had befallen since she had been gone. At the very least, they would afford her a bed for the night away from the chilling moan of the winter wind. With dizzy head and aching limbs she staggered on up to the house and, her hand shaking, she pushed open the door.

Chapter 4

FATE SHAPES ITSELF

THE cottage of the Elder was lit only by the ingle-blaze and three oil-wick lanterns upon the walls, carved into faces like luminous skulls. The atmosphere was fuggy with peat-reek, and close with the thoughts of the villagers, all huddled together in the one room. No one spoke, for they knew that Meggie was missing, and they were waiting for some sign as to why.

If for the Sidhe Samhain was the Feast of Life, for humankind, which sees reality from a different angle, it was the Feast of Death, when shades and fetches garb themselves in night shadows and come visiting. What were they to think, then, when the door opened and a cloaked figure, whose face and hands glowed phosphorescent green, crossed the threshold? For a moment no one dared breathe. The Old Woman broke the tension at last, by offering the apparition an ingleside seat and bringing it a little harp.

"Play," she said, without herself truly knowing the reason why.

Meggie's fingers ran automatically over the strings, plucking from them an exotic melody, outlandish sounding and yet as enigmatically familiar to the listeners as the sound of the wind in the trees or the corncrake in the grasslands. And then, although still unaware of what she was doing, she began to sing a curious little song.

Her song tailed off gradually as it triggered her mind to unwind its spinning whirl of unwoven images. She remembered first the parting words of the Queen, and then the tales and visions of lost times that had been revealed to her. She remembered the ethereal beauty of the Sidhe folk, and the breathtaking magnificence of their underhill hall. She remembered Annis, the old stranger who had led her safely there and back again, and finally she remembered who and where she was now.

"It is I, Meggie!" she cried suddenly, throwing back her hood. "I have returned!"

The villagers all jumped up to greet her, but the Old Woman waved them back with her hand. She knew from her own experience what it was like to journey between the worlds, and knew that Meggie must be given time to settle her senses and bring her experiences back to her present awareness.

"And where have you been, my Meggie?" she asked.

The words tumbled out wildly, without so much as a breathing-space, as the memories came alive again:

"Oh, I rode upon the back of a white horse that flew across the sky like a shooting star. I climbed down the inside of a mountain, and spoke to a great door of living wood. I danced to the music of the grass growing, and shaped the hills and valleys of the earth in the first ages. And the Queen of the Sidhe herself gave me a plate of beaten gold!"

She took the plate out of her shoulder-bag and unwrapped it with a flourish. But it had changed from fine polished gold into a dull thing of wood and, with a cry of bewilderment and disappointment, Meggie let it clatter to the ground.

* * *

Now, it is an ominous thing to reject a faery gift, the ill-effects of which can only be undone by an act of great love — if at all. For the love that is required entails a sacrifice that few have the courage to face, which changes forever the ways of weird of all those involved and alters irrevocably the

32

pattern of events that shapes the future of the world in which they live.

Neither Meggie who dropped the plate nor Gavin who picked it up again knew anything of the awesome fate which turned on that moment, for each simply acted as they must, without thought or reflection. But perhaps we, who can explore at leisure the far recesses of our imagination, can begin to understand why it is that their ancient land of Scotland is still a land of magic, still so close to the primaeval mists wherein lie the worlds of the Sidhe who shape the earth and all that lives and grows upon it. And perhaps some of us can, because of the events of that night, even now hear faery music on the Celtic winds and dance to the heartbeat of the land which is our mother too. It is for those that Meggie's song from the Sidhe is here recorded, for only they can turn the dead and inadequate written notes into the living beauty with which she sang it.

B

SIDHE SONG

Where the oakleaf trembles in a sunset beam,
The silvery salmon flashes in the stream,
The old stone toad does his bright eye gleam,
There do I await
To scatter stardust on mortal eyes
And show them the treasures of Nature wise,
That few remember when they rise
From their dreaming state.

Sunlight glinting dappled through the trees,
Still water rippling in a summer breeze,
Light and shadow playing, humming of the bees,
Call men to their fate,
Pull them, draw them from the day,
Through their own soul's longing sway
Their future from the cold, hard clay
That is their mortal strait. . . .

35

Chapter 5

PLATE AND CIRCLE

GAVIN was a strange one. He had been born in his mother's later years when his six elder brothers were already old enough to man fishing boats and mend nets. They were all broad shouldered and dark of feature, but Gavin, the seventh son, was small and slight, with a shock of bright red hair, and eyes of an unusually pale, clear grey. It was said, when he was born, that he would not last long upon the earth, so frail was he. But now he was in his fourteenth year, and during the summer had grown as tall as a man — taller indeed than most of the men around those parts.

He still had the unassuming manner of a child, though: he was awkward in his movements, and often blushed when he had to talk. He showed no inclination to follow his brothers to sea either. Instead, he spent his time whither he would, lending his hand wherever it was useful and asking no reward. He was clever with his hands, and inventive too, for never yet had there been any sort of repair or improvement needed that had been beyond his powers to carry out.

It was through his skill, rather than words, that he communicated, and he was never more eloquent than when he had a piece of driftwood in his right hand and a whittling knife in his left. He could carve the likeness of any animal or bird so well that he seemed to capture its life and its heart as well as its form, for he knew something of how to yield to the secret grains of his wood so that he harmonised his work with their natural beauty and flow. To him, each new piece of wood was a friend who communicated a unique character, challenged his understanding, and taught him ever more about his art.

When the wooden platter clattered to the ground, then, he instantly saw in it the golden treasure that Meggie had failed to see, and swooped to pick it up. He examined it closely, caressing its smooth texture in awe and admiration. The plate was of yew, and never before had he seen a piece of yew-wood of that quality or diameter. It was a rich golden-red, and had a most beautiful grain pattern that undulated gently like the folds of the glens sloping down to the sea from the northern hills. Its shallow bowl must have been turned using tools sharper and finer than he had yet made or come across, so silken was its feel and so even its gradation. And the matching of its contours to the curves of its grainflow was wrought with such an instinctive harmony that it sung to his sensitive eye like a tune upon the harp. Truly, this was the product of a master craftsman — a priceless treasure, and a continual source of joy and inspiration to the fortunate beholder.

In the meantime, while Gavin had been admiring the yewen plate, the Old Woman had been tending to Meggie, who had started shivering as if in shock after dropping it. A bowl of steaming posset had been brought for her to drink, and her limbs massaged with a herbal unguent to bring the blood back to the surface. There was nothing seriously wrong with her, of course — it was always like this when one was first called to awaken the erstwhile slumbering regions of the soul. It was like the ache of a muscle that is suddenly worked hard after a long period of laxity — it soon passes, and one is the healthier for it afterwards.

Now was not the time to press the issue of the plate, however, so she bade Gavin wrap it up and put it away safely when he offered to return it. There was other more urgent business to attend to before the night ended — the electing of the year's Circle.

The clachan consisted of a random scattering of cottages

through all the glens to the south of the Moothill that had access to the white-shelled bay. Each house occupied its own stretch of land, with neither track nor road to connect one to the other, but nevertheless the people thought of themselves as bound together, and worked communally to complete the seasonal tasks. This unity and harmony of purpose was most profoundly expressed in the Circle, elected each year at Samhain, after the signs and omens that accompanied the festival had indicated who should be chosen. The Old Woman chose three Maidens and three Mothers which, together with herself, made seven women. The Elder chose five other Mootmen to serve with him. Seven women and six men — thirteen altogether. No one knew why the Circle should take this form, save that it had always done so and that it always worked. It seemed right to follow the form of the Circle of Long Stones that surrounded the Moothill, for there were thirteen of them also.

The Circle attended to the ritual preparations for the festive Quarter Days, which realigned the people to the powers of Nature and the Elements that sustained them throughout the cycle of the year. Further than that, it was the special task of the chosen women to develop their skills of healing and divination, while the Mootmen took on the responsibility of the day-to-day affairs of the people, calling them to meet, resolving disputes, and carrying out business with itinerant strangers.

Upon the eve of each full moon, the whole Circle adjourned to the Long Stones to perform a ritual handed down from antiquity which had the power to make the Stones buzz with energy as a tree does, as if they were drawing goodness from the very moisture in the soil and the sunlight in the air. There was a saying among the people that they would prosper as long as the Stones lived, so the electing of the Circle was of the utmost importance to them.

The Old Woman chose first. Meggie was to be chief

Maiden, while the other two were younger girls whom Meggie could guide. Both Meggie's and Gavin's mothers were to be Mothers, along with a young woman who had just borne her first child. The Elder then chose his Mootmen, the last and youngest of whom was Gavin.

The business of the night now settled, the company fell to feasting the new year. Afterwards, they gathered round the hearth fire that was life to them while the sun was quenched by the Samhain night, and they whiled away the rest of the dark hours telling legends of long-dead heroes, singing ballads of ancient loves, and playing music together, to which they and the flames danced. But with the first pale rays of morning the feast of Samhain ended, and each of the company returned to their own home to prepare for the long winter of the new year.

Chapter 6

THE PLATE SPEAKS

A FTER Samhain, it was said, the plants and grasses were not fit to eat, for the goodness in them sunk like the winter sun below the surface of the earth to enrich the roots and seeds for the next spring's growth. The last of the berries and nuts had been picked the day before for the festival itself; anything left now belonged to the faery folk who had made it.

So it was now that the cattle and sheep had to be brought down from the pastureland where they had browsed on the sweet meadowgrass the summer long. They were taken indoors to the byres at the back of each house, and there they would spend the winter, feeding upon what hay had been gathered and dried in the sun when growth was good. Winter was a lean time for animals and people alike, when food and fuel had to be carefully conserved if they were to last: Samhain indeed marked the season where the borderline between life and death was thin, and the elements were at their most inimical.

The hours of daylight waned all the while, and had to be used to best advantage. The women would gather together to spin and weave, singing as they worked to keep their fingers nimble and their minds from the bitter cold that howled indoors through every crack. The men did repairs on house, furniture and boat, twined ropes and made tools. But all too soon the light would become too poor to work by, and for the long evening's darkness there was nothing to do but sit and stare at the pictures in the ingle-fire flames, using them to dream by. It was a time when new ideas and insights could crystallise, but nothing could yet start to grow into being. The fate of the future lay frozen and unborn like a seed within the dark, nourishing soil of past memories.

Gavin came over whenever he could to help Meggie understand the true nature of her yewen plate, so that by the wisdom of acceptance she would be able to see again the gleam of faery gold through its wooden surface. He explained that the sacred symbols the Queen had bade her carve upon the plate were within the wood itself, for all pieces of wood are naturally inset with such symbols by the spirit of the tree as it grows. In them, the tree instils the essence of its experience, the living runes of its history. To gain this hidden store of wisdom for himself, all the carver had to do was to allow the sacred symbols to reveal themselves, and then release their true forms by his art. Simple!

Meggie did not think so, however. She listened to Gavin's explanations again and again, but to no avail. Try as she might she just could not see anything in the wood at all beyond the curving lines on its surface. First Gavin would say that she was not looking with enough attention, then that she was trying too hard. You cannot *will* the symbols to appear, he would say, only allow them to. After a few weeks of this Meggie felt like screaming in frustration at the stupidity and futility of the exercise. Gavin was none too happy either: impatient that Meggie was so slow to pick up something so easy and obvious, irritated that he could not just save time by showing her the pictures which by now were leaping out of the wood at him screaming to be carved. If the truth were known, he was more than just a little jealous that it had been the unappreciative Meggie who had been given this priceless treasure, and not himself.

The tension between them exploded one day into an angry row. Gavin walked out of Meggie's house vowing never to help her again, and Meggie banged the plate down in the far corner of the dresser, determined to forget all this nonsense about the Queen Underhill and the sacred symbols. She set to work with a vengeance on a pile of wool that needed teazing and spinning, trying to convince herself that she wanted nothing more from life than the workaday routine. After about a week, her anger and frustration had subsided, and she was reconciled to the usual rhythm of winter life — spinning, weaving, and telling stories by firelight. She still had not spoken to Gavin since, but felt at peace with herself at least, and content with the comfort of normality. Life was as it should be.

It was just when she thought that the haunting dreams of Samhain had faded forever that it happened. As she walked past the dresser one morning, she suddenly seemed to catch the image of a bird out of the wick of her eye. Her spine tingling, she turned slowly round and scanned the whole shadowy area thoroughly, but could see nothing out of the ordinary. She retraced her steps and when the image reappeared, she froze. Fixing her eye upon it, she wheeled round to face it squarely. It was unmistakable. A tiny raven, scarcely moving as it hovered upon the wind, but alive for sure, flew towards an old Scots pine, upon, or rather within, the yewen plate. The image was steady and clear and only needed to be made real by her acknowledgement. Her heart beating fast, she fetched the sharpened tool of ram's horn that Gavin had given her to mark the plate, and tentatively outlined the raven and tree upon the wooden surface. The lines began to glow faintly green, and the animated images seemed to talk within her mind.

"I am the Raven, messenger of the gods. I bring from them your fate upon a platter. The one who sees an enemy before him will swim in his own blood in battle, but the one who sees only love knows that death is but a doorway. The roof of this tree is the roof of the world, and if you look from it as I do, you will know all things that need concern you."

Then it seemed as if the old pine spoke. It told of the soul of the land which it had guarded since its birth, the land of which Meggie was but a young child. As it described the secret life of that land, the images it evoked impressed themselves upon the wooden plate, and Meggie captured them swiftly and surely now with the ram's horn point. There was a hare, a hawthorn berry, a fulmar on a cliffside, a young doe in a forest, a high mountain, clover in the grassland, a coiled snake — a thousand little things. By the time the images faded, and Meggie laid down her tool to inspect the work, the plate was covered all over with a delicate tracery of fine green lines, similar to the patterns on the dome of the Hollow Hill.

For a little while she had no wish to share the secret of the plate. She kept it wrapped and hidden under the blankets of her bed, only bringing it out at night after she had drawn her bed-curtains to shut out the world. The green lines glowed strongly in the darkness, and she would lie awake for hours retracing them with her mind, picking out the interlaced images and letting them tell their own story.

It was after the Moothill ritual of midwinter, when the sun renews itself and light returns to the land, that she decided to tell Gavin at last that she had managed to carve the plate. He was surprised but pleased and, their quarrel forgotten, they walked back down the glen to Meggie's cottage together talking of the various symbols and what they meant.

When Meggie unwrapped the plate this time, though, all they could see in the pattern of green lines was the trunk and twigs of a yew — the tree that grows between the graves of lovers to keep them forever apart.

Part Two

The White Raven

Chapter 7

BRIGIT'S CRADLE

THE long, dark hours of winter were a time for rest and contemplation, but by and by a new wind stirred the frozen land. The animals began to sniff the air and paw the ground restlessly, while people's thoughts turned from the past to the future. The season of introspection was ending; the season of activity was beginning to unfold like the sticky new buds of spring. Slowly the snow released its icy grip upon the ground, and life yawned and stretched out of its hibernation.

Upon the eve of Imbolc, the women of the Circle met in Meggie's cottage to celebrate the festival of the returning light and the renewal of spring. The ritual was dedicated to Brigit — the triple Goddess who was Maiden, Mother and Muse — and was a woman's mystery. No man was ever allowed to attend.

First of all, the ingle-fire was banked as high and hot as it could be, and water freshly drawn from a hill-spring was put on to boil. Some was used to scour down the walls and furnishings of the house, before the remainder went into the tub, so that each of the women and girls could wash thoroughly. Then they loosed their long hair from its winter braids, and rinsed it in fresh water scented with yarrow and rosemary. Everything had to be pure and clean as a spring flower to welcome Brigit.

When they had dried before the fire, they all dressed alike in loose smocks of linen bound at the waist with a fine cord. Their legs, arms and heads were bare. After their heavy winter kirtles, shawls and stockings of dark wool, under-skirts of rough linen and leggings of leather, it felt strange and wonderful to feel their clean skin fresh against the fire-warmed air. It made them feel so light and free that their bodies wanted to soar into the air instead of walking, and their voices danced into song as they went about the evening's tasks.

The Old Woman bade the Mothers go to the back of the house to weave a cradle from the cornstalks of the last sheaf gathered from the previous harvest, while the Maidens stayed by the fireside to weave the likeness of a baby from osiers of willow. Meggie showed the two younger girls how to apply just the right amount of pressure to bend the pliant twigs firmly into shape without breaking, and they became quietly absorbed in the work as it took on the semblance of a living form. Just before they had sealed up the last holes with wicker weaving, the Old Woman stuffed the hollows with the dried white flowers of the hedgerow sacred to Brigit. Pearlwort, stitchwort, gowan and yarrow: all were blessed in her name and put in place.

When the willow-baby was finished, Meggie danced round it singing a curious song of invocation:

> "At the first pale light of dawn
> The cow fills with new milk for her young child,
> Likewise the white sap rises in the trees.
> Willow, willow wand
> You hold the secret of moon-swollen tides
> Within your veins,
> You whisper with the winds
> That life is born anew this day of spring.
> And as you breathe your news upon the air
> The serpent sloughs its winter skin,
> The raven wise begins to build its nest.
> The ice of winter loosens hold
> And melts into the springs,

The buds unfurl, the green earth sprouts again.
Willow, willow wand
You touch the poet's soul
And inspiration pours into his pen.
Willow wand I fashion you
As a blossom-child of spring
And Brigit name you — flow with life again!"

The movements of her arms as she danced garnered energy from the chant vibrating on the air and poured it into the wicker child. Thus did Meggie give it meaning and bring it life.

The Old Woman wrapped it in a clean white cloth, blew her breath of age and wisdom upon it, and, as tenderly as if it had been a child of flesh, she laid it on the corn-cradle, set upon a linen cloth in the centre of the scrubbed floor.

"The Spirit of Spring is born again," she said softly. "Who will bring her a gift to welcome her home?"

Each of them came forward in turn, and decorated the cradle with tokens they had collected in secret following the Old Woman's advice. The Maidens each brought three pebbles from the riverbed, as smooth and white as eggs. These were to represent the children of the Flowing Stream which was Brigit. The Mothers each laid down three white shells from the beach, which were like a mother's heart, for they had nourished and protected a creature born into the Sea of Life. Lastly, the Old Woman brought three white feathers. The first was Flight through which we rise above the troubles of earth, the second the White Bird of the soul, and the third pure Thought which uplifts and inspires. The feathers three she named and fastened to the hand of the willow-baby. Then she surrounded the cradle with nine white candles and lit them.

"Thrice seven gifts have we offered thee, and thrice three candles for thy halo of stars, Brigit the thrice-blessed."

The others looked on with silent pleasure at the simple

but awe-inspiring beauty of their creation. Brigit's Cradle seemed to tinkle and sparkle within the aura of the tiny candle-flames, radiating peace, and the hope of renewal after the devastation of winter.

When it was time, the Circle of women broke up and set about strewing the floor around the cradle with fresh rushes. The Maidens and Mothers settled down there to sleep in vigil over the baby until the morning sun replaced the lesser light of candles and stars. The Old Woman had other tasks. She smoored the fire, blessing it in the name of Brigit, protector of life, family and home. She raked smooth the ashes on the hearthstone on which Brigit might leave her mark. She set out a bowl of milk for the Child-Spirit, and put the household utensils in order. Meggie tried as hard as she might to keep awake so that she could see all the things the Old Woman did deep into the night, but her eyes were heavy with sleep and would not stay open. The last thing she heard was the Old Woman at the doorway calling into the darkness:

"Brigit, Brigit, thy bed is made ready. All is clean and new and awaits thy coming. Brigit, bless this household with thy presence, for thou art most welcome."

Chapter 8

AIRBORNE

MEGGIE opened her eyes again suddenly, though whether a few seconds or a few hours had passed since she had heard the Old Woman calling at the door she could not tell. The window was still dark with night and the others were fast asleep on the floor around her, but the air was sparkling silver and was scented with the sweet spring fragrance of apple-blossom. She sat bolt upright and looked round. Upon the threshold a young girl stood shimmering in pale pink light, the colour of dawn. Her features were fair and serene as a high-born lady, but she was dressed simply in a homespun robe and her flaxen hair flowed loose to her waist from a chaplet of flowers upon her head.

"Brigit!" Meggie gasped in astonishment. "Welcome art thou!"

The shining maiden smiled gently. "I am not she, though I bring with me her spirit to bless this gathering in her name. I am Annis, and am come to take you with me."

"Annis?" queried Meggie, a little irreverently. "But she is old and bent and grey, and you . . ." She trailed off there, realising that what she had said sounded rather insulting.

". . . and I am young and fair?" finished Annis in her place, with a mischievous twinkle in her eyes. "But don't you know, little Meggie, that the Goddess herself is ever-changing like the moon, and contains within her all the aspects of womanhood? Why, even Brigit of the Spring is at one and the same time the child being born, the mother giving birth, and the old wise-woman who attends as midwife. I come to you ever bedecked with the clothing of the season, for I come to you as herald of the season. But I came not to argue away the last hours of the night but to take you on a journey. Will you come with me, little one?"

Meggie rose from her place in silent assent and joined Annis on the threshold. When she looked behind her, though, she saw her body still lying sleeping on the floor with those of the other women, as motionless as stone. The sight did not alarm her, she noted, but she turned to Annis for an explanation.

"Do not worry, little friend. You do not need your cloak of flesh for this journey, for we travel on the air itself and must be lighter than air to do so. The blessing of Brigit will keep your body safe from harm until you return. Come!"

And as the smoke from a smoored fire curls in drifting trails, so they rose now upon the soft, still air, their loose hair fanning like unfurled wings behind them. Silently as thought they moved, thin as a breath they floated through the mantle of darkness while nothing stirred beneath them. Over the sleeping fields they passed, gliding above the snow-capped peaks of unnamed mountains, skimming the waves of the cold eastern waters. Upon the aromas of a foreign land upborne, onwards, onwards they soared: past shepherds on shady hillsides piping to their heedless flocks, past poplars dark and tall upon a new horizon, past cluttered red-tiled houses, cedars spreading, minarets and mosques mushrooming on unknown meadows.

Thought was their flight and thought their speed. Lightly they rode into the rosy light of dawn, and lightly they landed upon the Fair Plain of which the poets sing.

Chapter 9

IN PRAISE OF THE PLAIN
OF EVER-DAWN

FAIR is the Plain of the Ever-Dawn —
fairer than the skies upon a spring morning
over the land that we call home.
Like a woodland anemone
growing in a fallen log
is its pure, pale beauty
against the rough, dark earth.
Flowers star its gentle grasses,
and lush they sway from the heartland
to the salmon streams
sparkling with crystal life.
Healing herbs sing fragrance on its breezes,
trees with fine blossom hang heavy,
birds upon the wind carol in harmony,
bees dance drunk with nectar.
White hinds there are in the thickets
tending their young without fear,
rabbits on the grassland leap
and hares course free.
No want is there, but laughter
bubbles like a clear spring
endlessly from which we drink.
Songs are never far from our lips there,
nor happiness from our hearts.

Sweet are its waters like honey-mead,
Its green shoots tender on the tongue,
And when we breathe the light within its air
forever we stay young.

Chapter 10

APPLE BRANCH

THE two girls skipped across the verdant pastures like young lambs, chasing and tagging each other in light-hearted play. They collected flowers for Meggie's hair, nibbled savoury fronds of burnet and bergamot, and drank of the sparkling waters of the Flowing Stream. They went a-wobbling with new-born fawns, leaping with frogs, hopping with rabbits. Up and down the Plain they giggled and gambolled, while the dawn chorus sang their joy into the sky, painting it in a thousand pastel shades. Coming to life was a child's game, careless and free.

Then over the twitter and chirp of the fledgelings, the magical voice of the White Raven called them, softly but insistently. On the flow of its song they floated once more up into the air, gliding upon its notes to her great nest at the top of the highest tree. Gently they landed, and snuggled under her soft wings for comfort.

"I am the Soul of Brigit," said the White Raven, "and the Mother of Spring. Ever at Dawn I weave my nest from the stuff of life itself, so that Nature may be clothed in finery and the Earth dance in colour and light. Each branch and twig must be in its true place here, each sacred tree interwoven with care, that all in existence be maintained in vitality and harmony. See how the meshing branches form the matrix of life!"

She talked to them then of the sacred trees, which each have their appointed meanings and language, and explained how they worked with one another to maintain the fabric of

55

creation. She taught them how to hear a tree's song — its secret, tiny voice with which it communicates with the Cosmos and makes its surroundings hum with life — and how to talk to a tree so that it will tell you what you need to know. She showed Meggie then how to twine the tree-shoots into the curve of the nest, much as Meggie had shown the Maidens how to weave the Willow-Baby. Finally, she snapped off a little twig of apple, topped with white blossom, and presented it to Meggie, saying:

"Take this branch of the Sacred Apple Tree, and guard it well. The fragrance from its blossom is the life-giving wind of spring, and its fruits confer the gift of life on those who taste them with understanding. The music of the Apple is the tinkling of life in spring stirring into action. It is the sound of the birds and the lambs, of the mountain springs tumbling with the melting snows, the early insects, and the unfolding flowers. Should you ever need my help, wave but a branch from the Sacred Apple, and I will surely hear its song and answer the call. Fare you well, Meggie, and true be your thought."

Meggie thanked the Raven for the handsome gift, and, taking Annis's hand, she launched herself upon a morning sunbeam shooting at the speed of light far beyond the Plain of Ever-Dawn to the sleeping world in the west. As they approached Meggie's homeland, however, they could travel on the light no more, for the sun was still below the horizon. They felt themselves growing heavier and smaller as the light dimmed until, by the time they reached the village, they had shrunk to earthly size and landed upon the grass.

The sacred apple-branch in Meggie's hand had not shrunk with her, however, and was now too tall and heavy to carry. She set it down upon the ground in front of her cottage, where it instantly took root, so imbued was it with the vitality of its magical place of origin. In front of their eyes it grew into a beautiful tree, dripping in silvery-white blossom and mature fruit besides, tinkling melodiously in the eastern breeze. Meggie snapped off a flowering twig as a wand for the Willow-Baby, and went indoors. She turned upon the threshold and raised a hand in salute to Annis, who, shimmering pink and pale, melted away into the air as a star does at sunrise.

Meggie laid the apple-wand gently in Brigit's cradle, with a few whispered words of blessing and thanksgiving to the spirit of she who had given so much. Then she snuggled down into her body again, glad to fall into oblivious sleep in its heavy darkness upon the earthen floor. She slept soundly well into the morning, long after the others had woken and discovered the wondrous tree which grew where no tree had been the day before, and long after they had welcomed it into their midst by dancing and carolling around its trunk. No one had the heart to waken her, for her sleeping face looked so peaceful, its expression as innocent as a baby's. But even if they had called her, she probably would not have heard, for she was listening instead to a lullaby within her dreams, sung by the sweet voice of Brigit, the White Raven.

MEGGIE'S LULLABY

Sleep now, Meggie, like a babe after birth
Who drinks of the dew of the morning light.
A child in the heart of your mother the Earth,
While the last stars echo the songs of night.

Fair is the Plain of the Ever-Dawn,
Where the gentle hues of the sun-kissed sky
Are the scented petals that blossom its lawn,
And the eastern breeze on which dreams can fly.

59

Part Three

The Spiral Serpent

Chapter 11

BELTANE CROSSES

THE Apple Tree continued to grow and to flourish, and its fame spread far and fast. People would visit it from miles around to tell it their secrets, and tie on it a piece of cloth to flutter their wishes to the four winds and back again. Festooned with ribbons, blossoms, and fruit out of season, the sacred tree became a vision of beauty and of wonder which inspired all who beheld it, and brought a rare blessing upon the land.

On the morn of the full moon after the Vernal Equinox, the villagers gathered under the tree to bless the season's seeds before the communal planting. Whether it was the tree which bestowed on the seeds some of its own magic, or whether the people inspirited them with their own new-found vision of blossoming life, who could say? In any case, green shoots from all the crops were burgeoning tall, strong and healthy by the middle of April. The spring weather, too, was exceptionally well favoured, the days being long and fair and the winds gentle. The harvest promised to be most bountiful that year, and hopes ran high.

By the eve of Beltane the sun shone with the warmth of summer and the promise of bright days to come. Beltane was a special day for Meggie, when she and the other young girls would go with the flocks to the summer sheiling, the sweet meadowland on the hillsides above their homes. There they would stay in the bothies until the Samhain fires tolled the knell of the old year, and they returned again to the shelter of the stone cottages in the darkening glens.

Meggie loved the long, hot days of the sheiling, where she could take off skirts, tuck up petticoats and kick off shoes and stockings at last. Summer was sun-browned limbs, soft grass under bare feet, and sleeping under the stars. Summer was pulling fresh green herbs, flowers and shoots for salads, and dripping rich, creamy milk through muslin to make sweet cheeses. It was tending to the fattening flocks, churning butter, and dying, weaving and waulking woollen cloth in the open air together. And summer was long, light evenings when the young men would climb the slopes bringing food and ale, fiddles and pipes, to feast away the hours with the maidens until the sun finally sank below the horizon.

That was summer. Meggie could feel the pull of it in her bones and, like the animals, she could not sleep that Beltane night for excitement. But it was more than just the anticipation of summer that made her restless. It was the nearing of the strange dawn that lay between the night and the next day, with its hilltop need-fires of augury and archaic power, that now plucked her nerves like a note.

She got up and, by the light of a lamp, set about making bannocks for the morning on the last embers of the old fire. Before the family left the house to greet the sunrise, this fire, which had burned day and night in the hearth since Beltane last, would be put out and the ashes scattered. The light and heat of the fire was life to them, and its continuity as important as the rising of the sun each day. To put it out was an act of great faith that a new virgin flame could be lit to replace it, a flame full of the vigour of the strong, young sun that now disported in the sky. Until that happened, however, the old fire was still the guiding light of the household, and must be thanked and respected for its year's patronage. Meggie pulled off a part of the last bannock she was baking and cast it into the flames in dedication, saying:

"Blessed be, O chieftain of the flames. May thy hidden powers be passed on to thy son, our sun, this day, that we may have life and fire anew. Merry meet, merry part, and merry meet again."

She sprinkled water on the embers then to release the ancient spirit of the fire. He left with a loud sizzling sigh. Meggie felt alone and quite vulnerable. She quickly marked each of the warm bannocks with an equal-armed cross of protection so that the life-force would not leave them either, then set about making crosses of protection for the rest of the household.

From the twigs of rowan she had cut in the evening, she selected two long straight sticks, trimmed them into equal lengths, and notched them in the centre so that they fitted together smoothly at right angles. This equal cross she bound over and under round the centre with a cord of scarlet wool she had spun and dyed herself in a secret mixture of lichens the Old Woman had shown her. It was not everybody who could achieve a clear scarlet when they dyed. The nearest was the brownish crotal-red, and many attempts to improve on that failed. The secret was in the 'knowing': a matter of feeling inside yourself just what proportions of lichens would be right and just how often and how long to immerse the wool in the dye liquids. The pure scarlet achieved was the mark of magical prowess, therefore, and highly prized for its powers.

As she bound the crossed twigs with the scarlet cord, Meggie intoned a rune over them to concentrate her intent:

> "Rowan twigs with berry red
> Bound around with scarlet thread
> Pointing North, South, East and West,
> The Quarters four from which we're blessed
> By Earth and Water, Fire and Air:
> O Ancient Four be charged to spare
> The lives and luck of all who pass
> Beneath this sign of Beltanemas!"

c

Finally, she tied the wool into a loop, and hung the cross from it on a hook in the rooftree above the doorway. There it twirled round and back again to all the directions, in the early morning breeze that filtered in the crack between door and wall. The whole household, people and animals alike, would have to walk under this threshold cross on the way to the Beltane fires. It was a strong protection for them all.

By this time the rest of the family were up and about, and together they made other tiny crosses of rowan and red thread. Meggie fastened string to some to tie to the animals' tails, and long loops of red cord to others to hang round their own necks. As an extra precaution for herself, she consecrated her own neck-cord with knots, invoking all the names of light, life and love that she knew as she pulled each knot tight. Only after completing nine such knots did she begin to feel at ease, and then she fastened the cord to the cross at once and hung it round her neck next to her skin.

Chapter 12

LIGHTING THE NEED-FLAME

THE crosses made, the hearth swept clean and the bannocks wrapped in linen cloths to keep them fresh, Meggie and her family stepped out into the pre-dawn chill of the May morning, driving the animals before them. Silently they walked the straight track to the Moothill, and from every other cottage in the glens the same procession began, each family upon their own path converging on the mound within the Circle of Long Stones.

The Mootmen had already assembled there some hours previously to build a huge bonfire of timber specially selected from the village store. Wood from all the sacred trees was included, but precious branches of juniper and cedar from across the far seas had pride of place, for their fragrance as they burned had a powerful effect on the senses. The bonfire was circular in shape and divided into four by two wide paths in the shape of a cross. The Mootmen stood now in the central space where these paths met, putting the finishing touches to the device which would bring the need-flame to life. It was in the form of a six-spoked wooden wheel, its centre stuffed with dried grasses and other kindling, tightly fitted round a tall wooden stake stripped of bark and planted in the ground at the very centre of the mound. Each of the Mootmen would grip a spoke of the sun-wheel and drive it round and round, until the chafing of wood on wood gave off sparks and lit the kindling. If all went well, their virgin flame would have its birth just at the magic moment when the rising sun shot its first beams of light across the horizon to meet them. Then would earth and sky, man and god, be truly one.

In the meantime, the others formed an outer circle round the girth of the mound, just within the Long Stones. The Mootmen in the centre now started to hum upon a single note; the girth circle responded on a higher note. It was held until the very air seemed to vibrate in harmony. Then a chant began in the centre and spread outwards to the edges: a chant for the potent Sun to rise and light their lives once more, to send down his vital spark to quicken and regenerate themselves, their animals, land and crops. Louder and now quieter came the chant in waves of its own making, sounding and resounding within the open space of the circle. Then with one accord the Mootmen began to spin sunwise with the wheel, slowly at first, then gaining speed. The girth circle too now began to rotate, circumambulating the boundary of the sacred space and containing its power.

Faster and faster they went, circling and chanting, till it seemed to Meggie that the bonfire stack on the hill and the people around her became but a blur of unreality. Round and round she raced on the chant till her whole being seemed to pulse and quicken, quivering in response to an energy not her own that was filling her, and absorbing her into itself.

Suddenly a great glow rose from the hilltop: the bonfire had been lit from the need-flame! The chanting died down and, like the others, she slowed down and stopped circling, sinking to put her forehead on the ground in order to recover her balance and focus her eyes.

Chapter 13

SERPENT POWER

M EGGIE raised her head. The Moothill and Stones were the same as ever, but instead of the villagers in their coloured woollen clothes, she was surrounded by tall strangers, dark of feature and majestic of bearing. They wore long robes of white fastened with jewelled brooches, and circlets of gold upon their brows. Gold and silver bracelets spiralled up the arms of the women, while intertwined bands of coloured metals were neck torcs for the men. Meggie had never seen adornments so exotic, not even when ships from the southern lands moored on their isolated beach to trade, but she knew instinctively that these people were priests of some power and distinction. She got up hastily, almost embarrassed at having intruded on their ritual, but she was still too dizzy from the circling to stand. The ground seemed to spin up to meet her face, and her eyes saw only its blackness.

When she came to a few seconds later she was cradled in the arms of a priestess, whose high-arched cheekbones and finely chiselled features gave her face a striking, piercing air. Her gold circlet rose in filigree plumes above coils of braided black hair looped around her head, and her eyes were extended to the side like a cat's with paint of green malachite and kohl. But despite an unfamiliar appearance, the light in those eyes was unmistakable. Meggie managed a smile for her friend.

"Still your mind, my sister," said Annis, "and your strength will return. You have travelled a long way, but have still further to go upon the path of daring before this day is done. The sun is rising now, and his Serpent lies coiled in a circle of gold. Look up!"

Meggie looked up to the top of the Moothill as Annis pointed. It blazed more brightly than the morning sky, but there was no bonfire burning there at all. The flames simply poured like a fountain from the centre of the mound itself, leaping straight into the air and cascading out in six great streams. Through the dazzle she was just able to make out the forms of six priests upon the hilltop, whose chanting drew the light from earth and sun alike and channelled it through their upheld arms into its new form. The six streams of light arched high over their heads and came down to ground round the Long Stones, where they flowed into a circle that gleamed like gold. The liquid light-energy of the circle was then concentrated and shaped from without by the girth circle of priests who stood, man and woman alternately, holding hands and humming on harmonic tones. Even as Meggie watched, the circle began to thicken, then shimmer and writhe as if it had substance and form of its own. It was coming to life.

"Come," said Annis, "let us rise with the Serpent."

* * *

Annis walked to the southernmost point of the golden circle and, sounding an incantation in a language unknown to Meggie, she cast her right hand into it, closing in her out-stretched fingers as if compressing its light to a point. She held still for just a moment, sounded one last, long note, then withdrew her hand and stepped back beside Meggie. The Serpent's head began to take shape from the point that Annis had drawn: the tapered snout, the jaws slightly parted to accommodate the end of his own tail held in his mouth, the smooth elongated forehead, the fanned-out neck ruff. The two slant eyes smouldered red; the nostrils breathed fire.

Annis and Meggie climbed on just behind his head, and wrapped their arms securely round his long, thin neck. The Serpent's head waved from side to side as if adjusting to the weight of his passengers, then his jaw dropped slowly, and the arrowhead tail fell out on to the ground. The priests increased the pitch of their hum until the air around them wavered like a heat haze. The Serpent arched his neck high in response, breathed out a cloud of flame, and at last lurched lazily upwards into the sky.

Six times the Serpent spiralled, Meggie counted; for six times she saw the white-shelled beach to the south spin by her. Each time it seemed smaller and further away as they rose higher. Now she could see all the glen beneath her as she looked out, but directly below was the golden circle of priests round the Moothill, still sending waves of liquid light up the spiralling path to meet them. Then the Serpent stopped rising, but turned slowly in a seventh circle, until his head finally met his own back. It rested there for a split second, then fused with itself into another golden circle. Immediately a blinding arc of light flashed above and below it, and took form.

The seventh circle contained a shining egg suspended high above the Moothill on the conical spiral of the Serpent, and the shining egg contained Annis and Meggie.

Chapter 14

ALBINA

THE inside surface of the egg was faceted with innumerable tiny hexagons, each acting as a prism to split the light into its many colours and back again. They gave the illusion of great space, for indeed it was hard to tell where light became surface and surface light. Reflections seemed to bounce into infinity; recognisable shapes formed and instantly dissolved again as the focus of light and colour altered. Who knows how long it took for Meggie and Annis to fathom the secrets of the mirrored globe?

Eventually they learned not to follow the chimeric images of pathways arched by serpents of light, and not to shrink from the distorted faces of wild beasts spouting fire that loomed and leered at them fleetingly from the reflecting surfaces. Instead, they stilled their minds, until the images settled; then they concentrated their vision with determination, until the walled surfaces became clear. They walked once round the periphery to establish its definite limits, then spiralled inwards to its centre.

They came upon the White One suddenly. Her features were barely distinguishable from the surrounding lightscape, but there was no ignoring the sultry power of her presence, nor the burning intensity of her gaze. Meggie felt as if she would be drawn in and consumed by that gaze, which stripped every nerve-ending raw, and confounded all resistance. Her only possible defence was to match and reflect it. She felt herself shake as she summoned energy from every fibre of her being with words of power that came to her instinctively, though she had not heard them before. Power rushed upwards to her head. Her mind seemed to surge briefly with an exquisite vibrancy, exulting in its own omnipotent freedom, until its desire turned it excruciatingly inwards upon itself. Sparks flew as energy ground against energy, will against will. Hope and fear fused into a single perception which embraced eternity. Meggie's mind became a white-hot point of searing concentration. Her need-fire was alight.

She raised her eyes at last to meet the gaze of the White One, whose form now appeared unveiled before her. Her face had not the fey beauty of the Sidhe of the Hollow Hill, nor yet the innocent freshness of the Imbolc Maiden. It was long and sleek, with the feral majesty of a wild horse, proud and free. Her complexion was an incandescent white, as were her flowing robes of woven light. Her long hair, and the plaited girdle round her waist, were of fine strands of brilliant red-gold. She did not move or speak, but seemed to communicate upon subtle pulses of light that shone from her hypnotic eyes. Meggie felt the words exploding and resounding inside her mind in extravagant splashes of bright colour.

"This is the Temple of Fire, formed of the Light which is Life, and I am the Altar at its Heart. My name is Albina. I am the White Spirit of the fire which resides in your land, which the mighty ones called Alba in remembrance of me. I am the fire in the hearts of the people of Alba, and the light in their eyes."

The White One raised her upturned hands in offering towards Meggie. Their luminosity flickered like firelight, then extended out into the form of a chalice, or bowl, or maybe a flower — the rays of light of which it was composed were so fine that Meggie could never be sure, her senses being too dull and slow to take in the ephemeral image. But whatever its form, it soon became clear that its radiant point lay at its centre, where the liquid white light now collected and concentrated, pulsing like a heart. Gossamer strands of golden-red sprayed out from this centre. Like threads they wove the fabric of the cup, then spilled out over it to encircle and permeate the globe of the temple. From there, they seemed to fan out in all directions: a golden web of life sustaining the whole of creation.

The White One reached inside the cup and picked up the radiant centre in her fingertips, holding it out towards Meggie. Again she did not speak, but the essence of her words washed through Meggie's senses like the perfume of a flower on a summer day.

"This is the Jewel of the Heart, beyond price and beyond description. It is a great and fearsome weapon, so do not use it without love. By its power all things melt, and are won." So saying, she pressed the pulsing jewel of liquid light against Meggie's own heart, and her body absorbed it instantly, without resistance.

Golden-red rays shot through her being. Golden-red rays pulsed and spurted through her veins like blood. Golden-red rays wove over and under the separate elements within her like a scarlet cord, binding and bonding them into a central unity. The power of the fusion exploded and radiated like a sun from her heart. Meggie shone with white fire. She was the Centre of the Universe, the Fount of Life, the Crux or Cross of Creation! She lifted her hands to hold those of Albina. They were one now: the Altar at the Heart of the Temple of Fire. The Temple was their aura, the endless outpouring of the fire within them. Serpents hissed and coiled around them. Salamanders wriggled and darted. Dragons snorted and roared. Meggie breathed fire through every pore. She was alive and burning!

Then somewhere, somewhere quite unfathomable in the midst of the boundless white fire, a tiny black cinder appeared like a sunspot. Meggie ignored it and carried on burning euphorically. It insisted; it would not go away. Meggie blasted it with a dart of supreme white fire. The black spot grew. Meggie began to be uncomfortably aware of her own fallible self again, and she was extremely angry. How dare this blot intrude on her cosmic consciousness, and undermine her crucial role in the great work of creation!

"I am your destiny," said the black spot. "You cannot escape me."

Meggie felt her mind trembling, and she lost her grip on Albina's hands. The black spot grew into an enormous hole and Meggie tumbled in. She heard herself calling to Annis for help, and was dimly aware of the wise one's arms encircling the blackness that engulfed her. The harmonic hum of the ancient priesthood contained and protected them both.

She decided after a moment's struggle to trust her safety to Annis and the priests, and to submit to the fall. Her anger and pride began to melt away then, and was absorbed by the soft, comforting darkness. It felt good to be no longer responsible, to relinquish decision, to be empty and free. The universe could carry on without her now. Oblivion felt far better than burning. Meggie snuffed out her need-fire and returned to her senses.

Chapter 15

MAY DAY

"MEGGIE, Meggie, my love, come, come!"
Someone was holding her hands and calling her.
"Albina?" she wondered aloud, opening her eyelids with difficulty and squinting through the dazzle of sunlight.

"What are you blethering about, child?" chided her mother gently. "The Fire of Beltane is within you, that's all. We have all been blessed by the Sun upon and within us. There's no need for you to get so carried away! Come to the feasting with us."

Meggie looked around, and realised with embarrassment that she was the only one left standing in the central space on top of the hill. The fires around her had died down by now, and the rest of the people were sitting about outside them, toasting their bannocks and collops in the glowing embers. The smell of cooking food made her feel suddenly ravenous. She ran out gratefully to consume her portion of the feast from a more inconspicuous position, amidst the teasing laughter of her friends.

It was a lazy, self-satisfied morning. The ceremony had gone very well by all accounts. That, and the warm sun, made everyone feel good. No one was in a hurry to get on with the rest of the day. After a while, some of the girls went leaping over the balefire embers hand in hand with their beloved. The couples then blessed each other with a kiss and enveloped themselves in the loving secrets of each other's arms. Some, oblivious to the onlookers, walked away

76

together to the glens, but no one called them back to attend to their duties. It was understood that the fires of love alight within them called them away on another quest this day, no less important.

Meggie, full of food, lay on the grass sighing with contentment. The memory of Albina and the Temple of Fire was fading fast like a dream after wakening, but who cared? Life was too beautiful today to chase after spirits and shadows. Life was here to be enjoyed.

It was close to midday by the time everything was tidied away at last and everyone ready to go. Meggie and the other maidens rounded up the cattle and sheep to drive them up to the sheiling. It was easy work for once, for the animals too seemed to have caught the Beltane spirit after having been driven through the purifying fires. They were docile and amenable to the girls' cries. Up they went like a dream, their crosses of rowantree still dangling from their tails behind them.

Some of the men followed after, leading ponies pulling carts piled high with the things the girls would need for the summer. There was clothing and bedding, food and cooking-pots, wool and spindles, butterchurns and cheese-makers. Summer was not all play, even for young girls!

Their first task on arrival at the wooden hill-huts was to gather bushy heather twigs to fill the bedframes. It was a long job, made lighter by song. Next they had to sweep the earthen floors, make the beds, and set their belongings in order. The men in the meantime inspected the huts for winter damage, mending little holes with heather thatch and clay wherever they could. Permanent repairs could come later. The cows were then milked and supper made.

After work was finished for the day, there was still a scant hour left before sundown. Meggie, still bouncing with energy, wanted to use it to explore. She walked out alone and, delighting in the springy feel of hill-turf underfoot, climbed high and fast up the slope until she could look down on the Moothill. Thin wisps of smoke were still rising from the charred remains of the balefire. Its form — a circle quartered by a cross — was quite unmistakable from this angle, and the evening shadows of the thirteen Long Stones fell about its feet as if in adoration. Something tugged at her memory, but would not show its face. It irritated her and she could not settle. Turning her back on the scene, she walked behind a line of whin bushes that screened the Moothill from view.

Something glanced sunlight into her eyes. It was a small rock crystal, its irregular facets weathered smooth and clear. As she turned it over curiously in her hands, the burning red of the sinking sun echoed the White One's words within her mind: "This is the Jewel of the Heart, beyond price and beyond description". Fine strands of golden-red seemed to arc momentarily from sun to crystal, and beam from her heart to head, hands and feet, linking her to sky, sun and earth alike. She remembered in a flash. So the need-fire was not just a dream faded and gone into the ashes of the past; it was still alive and within her.

She was not sure exactly what it all meant, but knew that the feeling was precious and marked her as different and special. It would be best now if she never allowed herself to forget it. The rock crystal — although no fine thing like the real Jewel, of course — would serve as a keepsake. She would wear it next to her skin against her heart, where the real one was embedded. Maybe, in time, she mused, the pulse of the one within would magnetise the one without. Then it could be used as a charmstone for healing and protection, to spread her power of golden fire into the world. How right it felt!

Just then an evening breeze blew chill, reminding her that it was sunset. She pocketed the crystal and bounded back down the slope to the huts. By the time she got back, Gavin had just arrived to watch the flocks for the night. She showed him the rock crystal and asked if he could make a clasp for it so that she could wear it round her neck. He hummed and hawed and frowned, turning it round and round.

"*Very* difficult," he concluded, shaking his head. "Don't think it can be done."

Meggie was on the brink of telling him how important it was to her, but was at a loss for words. She was not sure she was even allowed to tell anyone else of her experience. They might not believe her, or, worse still, might even make fun of her because of it. There was nothing she could do. She humphed in irritation for the second time that evening, turned on her heel and stalked into the hut. People — well, Gavin in particular — could be so difficult!

Chapter 16

MEGGIE AND GAVIN GROW TOGETHER

MEGGIE woke up the next morning to find a circlet of buttercups on her pillow. Inside was the crystal, bound around with fine golden wire. Gavin had twined two long, thin strands of the precious metal together, and looped it round the crystal in six smooth arcs. The loose ends were gathered at the top and twisted into a golden circle. It was perfect! How could he have known?

She took the scarlet cord with the nine knots from around her neck and removed the rowan cross from it. As she threaded the cord through the golden circle, she thought fondly of the Gavin who had made it with such love and care in the middle of the night. She thought of his eyes as keen as a may-hawk's, his fingers as nimble as the limbs of a young deer, his hair that matched the sun for brightness. Her own spun thread lay entwined now in his coiled wire, and the crystal brought the blessings of both Sun and Earth for the joining of the two. She would wear it always. Perhaps, she dreamed contentedly, she and Gavin would jump over the Beltane fires together some day and share the secrets of love. In the meantime, though, love seemed to pour out of her like a fountain to all that lived.

She jumped straight out of bed and ran to seek out Gavin, but he had already left the sheiling for the low glens. No matter. She would go after him. With only her white linen petticoat on, she raced impulsively down the hillside, shouting his name until she was quite out of breath. Gavin sauntered casually out of the woodstore.

"What's up with you, Meggie?" he asked in mock surprise.

"Thanks!" gasped Meggie, between gulps of air. Gavin stared blankly. "For the clasp on the crystal, I mean!" she continued.

"Oh that," replied Gavin dismissively. "It was nothing."

"But it's beautiful," insisted Meggie, "really, really beautiful."

"Always knew you had no taste!" he teased, ducking behind the door as Meggie threw a clod of earth at his head.

"You're impossible!" she shouted.

"You're not so possible yourself, sometimes!" he grinned, popping his head back out again. "You should see the airs and graces you put on when you think you know best!"

Meggie blushed scarlet, for she knew that what he said was true. She might have the priceless Jewel in her heart, but she still had a lot to learn about humility before she could wield its power. Gavin was a hard teacher.

"Thanks anyway," she said more quietly. "I really do mean it, you know." She turned quickly and scurried back up the hill again before he could get a last word in, feeling small and silly for coming out in her petticoat like that. What would he think!

Gavin thought very highly of her as it happened, but he was not going to let her know that just yet. It could put all sorts of daft ideas into her head. She was a terrible one for dreaming anyhow, he argued to himself. He grinned broadly at nothing in particular, and whistled a merry tune all morning as he sorted and restacked the woodpile.

* * *

The first part of summer went on as well as it had begun. The sun shone continuously, and the workload was thus made light and pleasant. Plants, animals and people alike seemed to thrive on it. Spirits were high. No one seemed able to remember a better year at all.

As the warm, daylight hours stretched on into late evening, Gavin and Meggie spent more and more time together. They were a motley pair indeed — he tall, fair and a joker by nature; she small, dark and broody — but although they were both fiercely independent and often quarrelled, there was a curious affinity that drew them close, like a secret understanding that no one else could share.

Sometimes they would walk for hours on the purple hills in silence, with nought but a thought to bind them. Then would the company of the other seem but a poignant reminder of each one's own aloneness, felt deep inside amidst a community of human friends. Then would the landscape touch them softly, filling their emptiness with its fleeting beauty, reminding them that reality was change, and not constancy. They would see the kestrel hover only to swoop again, hear the plover's wistful cry echo and fade, feel like a feather a wisp of cloud stroke the sun and melt into blue, watch frail flowers wilting in unaccustomed heat. These things they shared in still, quiet places that words would have profaned.

There were other days when they jumped and yelled to the swish of waves on the white-shelled beach. Tumbling and fighting they went like fox-cubs, splashing and nipping like crabs in the shallows, diving like seals underwater, screaming like gulls as they surfaced, waving their tentacles like urchins in the air. Gavin had never trusted water deeper than his knees, but soon learned to swim after Meggie had pushed him in from the rocks a few times!

He got his own back by teaching Meggie to fish in the burn. Gavin could charm trout from the water with but a flash of his eye, it seemed. Meggie, on the other hand, if she ever did catch one — after hours of frenzy and losing her foothold on the riverbed pebbles more times than she cared to count — would be sure to lose it again by leaving it where it could flip itself straight back into the water. The more frustrated she got, the more Gavin would taunt her. He was impossible, there was no doubt about it! It took her a long, long time to realise that, if she could only laugh at herself, Gavin would stop teasing at once and laugh with her. After that, she caught quite a lot of fish without any trouble at all.

She asked him then to show her how to carve, for she had made such a good job of the faery plate, she felt, she surely had the gift for it as well as he. Gavin showed her how to handle knife and wood with care and feeling. The rest, he said, was up to her. With grim determination she set to it every morning as she watched the flocks, and every morning she ended up with a collapsed heap of wooden bits. For several days she said nothing to Gavin of her attempts and hid the sorry remnants under a bush where he would not find them. She persisted, though, until it finally dawned on her what she was doing wrong. She was trying to carve as Gavin carved instead of finding her own style. Perhaps her creations were *meant* to have a hole in the middle, even as Gavin's were meant to be solid and smooth.

She selected a new block of wood and tried again, this time yielding to the pressure that had broken her other blocks into bits, instead of straining away from it. She let the knife work as it would, without imposing her ideas on it through her fingertips. Shavings pared away recklessly from the hole in the centre, until it seemed that, even with the best will, it was bound to collapse in on itself yet again. And so it did, but this time instead of a heap of bits, she was left with four circles of wood, each interlaced within the other. She was thrilled and amazed at her achievement, for she had never seen wood carving like this before. So this was her style: an abstract one like the signs on the Long Stones, hinting at the Powers beyond the manifestations of nature, instead of imitating its forms as Gavin did. Although it was unusual, it was a true style and surely worthy of merit in its own right. It was her invention.

She set to work again to perfect the piece, smoothing and polishing the four circles of wood, and peeling them away

83

finely from underneath until each fitted neatly on top of the others, so that they could be stacked or taken apart at will. It was a work of genius. Even Gavin the Carver would have to admit that!

And so he did, when he climbed up the slopes to meet her that afternoon. Not only that, he sang her praises endlessly, calling her a true craftsman, born to carve. Meggie's heart beamed with pride. At last, she felt, she was as good as the Gavin who always seemed to be in the limelight. No more would she stay unrecognised and awkward in his shadow, for she had talents too.

The next day he brought her something he had made that night. It was a whole lattice of interlaced circles that did not collapse and stack as Meggie's did, but braced against each other into the form of a hollow globe. He had not simply pared away the centre to nothing either. Instead, he had captured the forms of three tiny birds in the heartwood by inserting a tool through the latticework holes. It seemed as if the three birds were forever flying in the eternal space of their delicate cage.

"A present," said Gavin, kneeling before her, "from the humble apprentice, to the true craftsman who showed him so much more than he knew about his art."

Meggie bit her lip and fought back the tears of confusion that were stinging her eyes. Did he always have to mock her so? Did he always have to make everything she did look so worthless in comparison to his own? Was there no end to the scope of his taunting? On the other hand, she had to admit, the gift was handsome and perhaps, just perhaps, it was offered in the spirit of the genuine love and admiration he had expressed for her work the previous day. Should she feel indignant or delighted? She swithered for a moment on the edge of hot indignation, but knew that if she indulged in it Gavin's sharp wit would hurt her even more. She decided, for once and for all, that delighted was the best way to feel.

It was Gavin's turn to feel embarrassed and confused next

when he received a generous hug and kiss in return for his gift. Tears of joy were streaming down Meggie's face. He knew then that she had learned her lesson so well, he would have to humble his own pride from now on if he wanted to keep up with her.

Part Four

The Isle of the Blessed

Chapter 17

MEGGIE'S SECRET

W HEN she was alone on the hillslopes, Meggie would dance like a bird sings. It was as if the thrum of the moorland wildlife, and the distant boom of the waves on the rocks below, set up a music within her to which her body curled and stretched in abandon. She had learned no steps, but her instinctive movement was the ancient creation dance of the Mother of the Earth. Its drumbeat was the pulse of Nature breathing, and its melody the shapes and colours of Nature's fruits. The power of her dance was so intense that it was a secret kept even from herself. No one else was ever meant to see it.

Gavin discovered her secret quite unintentionally one oppressively hot afternoon in mid-July. He had left her lying in the sun on the machair while he combed the rock-pools for crabs. He had meant to return by way of the white-shelled beach where she would have seen him coming, but some inexplicable urge made him wade past it, pushing through the shallow water to the west. He scaled the cliff-face at last, and approached Meggie from behind.

Her unmistakable silhouette, etched darkly against the horizon of the sea and sky, was writhing like an undine of the water, undulating like a wraith of the air. It was an ethereal and mysterious sight, completely enthralling. Gavin stood rooted to the spot, unable to either move or speak, while the vision danced on between the worlds, unaware of the spy in the grass.

Meggie's voice danced too, swooping and soaring like a

gull on the wing. The notes had an unearthly purity, infused with a primal meaning that transcended the limitations of words. Gavin felt them touch him somewhere beyond the level of his comprehension, in a way that he had never been touched before. The tiny hairs on the back of his neck began to stand on end and his whole spine tingled. He got the distinct feeling that no one could look as boldly as he upon this dance, nor listen as openly to these sounds, and live. Something seemed to break inside him then. The boundaries of his reality shattered like glass. His legs shaking, he turned and ran, diving headlong from the clifftop into the shock of cold water. It was some time before he could summon up enough courage to walk up the white-shelled beach and face Meggie again.

When he eventually did, she was lying in the machair exactly where he had left her, smiling at him through drowsy eyes.

"Are you back already, Gavin Crabhunter?" she murmured. "It is surely just a wee moment since you left."

"You must have been sleeping, Meggie," replied Gavin softly, his throat dry and his voice faltering. "Did you go a-dreaming I wonder?"

"Och, no," said Meggie. "I was too tired for that, I'm sure."

Chapter 18

MEGGIE UNVEILED

THAT evening the heavens opened and rain poured down in torrents. Meggie was alone in her sheiling hut, cocooned in the interminable hiss of water falling on wood. Through the window she saw the sky turn livid again and again as lightning ripped the dark clouds to tattered shreds. Thunder crashed assertively, then ominously rumbled away like a growling dog guarding its territory. The storm must have been virtually overhead.

Meggie's head, pounding from her afternoon sleep under the glaring sun, fretted over the hasty message that Gavin had left her with as they went their separate ways that afternoon, anxious to reach shelter before the storm broke. "You're not just a carver or a fisher like me. Yours are the lost Arts: Dance, Poetry and Song. Find them, Meggie!" he had said urgently, gripping her shoulders tightly.

She paced up and down the tiny hut now, pulling and tugging at her mind as if to wrest from it by force the meaning of his cryptic words. How could dance, poetry and song ever be lost? They were as natural as breathing to the people of the Long Stones. Everyone used the rhythms of song and dance to work and play by every day; everyone could make up new rhymes for the fun of it. It was something the people did together, so how could Gavin say that these things were hers alone? And if they were really lost, where could she begin to look for them?

She felt her mind reach a frenzy at last in its demand for answers, stabbing like jags of freakish lightning into her unfathomed darkness, while the guardian dog of her deep secrets growled menacingly from within. Her feet, unheeded, were stamping out on the earthen floor the rhythms of her pounding head, her arms flailing like storm-tossed trees around her. So she moved on in the timeless storm of her mind, to the wild music of the storm outside.

Who could say whether she would have discovered her answers at all, if there had not been a sudden, eerie calm as the eye of the outer storm passed overhead? The eye brings understanding, it is said. Thunder, wind and lightning ceased abruptly and, to the hiss of the still-falling rain, Meggie found her body dancing a storm all by itself, her lone voice a startling ban-sidhe's wail in an unknown tongue.

She knew at once then only too well what Gavin had meant. Her arts were lost because she had not known she possessed them, and hers alone because they were different from the communal ones of her people. They were secret Arts that contained her Power: her Power to invoke the elements — and to raise storms. Appalled and stunned at what she had unwittingly done, Meggie sank to her knees and called out to Annis to help her, begging that this burden of Power be lifted from her so that the storm could cease. There was a dreadful moment of silence, then, in a voice formed from the encircling hiss of rain, Annis answered:

"Your burden is not Power, but your denial of Power, and your false shame at its discovery. These are the emotions which seethe within you now with the turbulence of a storm. I cannot lift them from you as you ask, but you can let them drain like water into the earth beneath to nourish the hidden roots of plants. Let the storm go, gentle Meggie."

Meggie felt her limbs and her mind grow heavy. The beaten earth floor felt soft and yielding now as she relaxed completely and lay down on it. Her eyelids drooped lazily; her thoughts drifted. Upon the brink of consciousness she felt the voice in the rain continue:

"You are not a child of the storm, and neither is the storm your child. For together you danced in the first ages before your mind became proud and distant. In the deeps of the first ocean you were one, and you were born together from its primal waters. You are the twin children of Chaos and of Night, from which all the beauties of creation sprang, and now you will return together unto the blessed darkness of your source, to know once again the peace of belonging. . . ."

If there was more Meggie did not hear it, for she was now in a sleep too deep and too still even to dream.

* * *

She woke early the next morning, completely refreshed. Outside, the sun was rising into a sky so cloudless and blue that it was hard to imagine the night's dark storms had ever been. The plants around looked lush, full and vivid green after their long soaking, and even the mountain rocks sparkled bright and clean. Meggie breathed in the sweet smell of the warm, damp earth with satisfaction. The world looked very beautiful to her today.

She completed her morning tasks quickly, then went to find Gavin. She knew what she had to do. Without any explanation, she led him away into the woods, brushing past the trees through long, wet grass and dewy sorrel. They came at last to an open glade whose flowery meadow now steamed exotically under the high noon sun. She bade Gavin sit on a stone, stepped forward from him just a few paces into the enigmatic haze, then paused to drink in deep the heady atmosphere of fragrance and birdsong. When she felt it begin to move her, she gave her consent and started her secret Dance with full awareness for the first time.

To begin with she found it difficult to let go fully, so conscious was she of Gavin's two eyes upon her back. She felt that if she did, they would bore right through her Dance and expose her naked soul, the thought of which frightened her still. Her painful shyness made her movements awkward and stiff. A few times it got so bad she had to stop altogether and take long, deep breaths until she could allow the inner rhythms of nature to move her gracefully once again. She would not give up, though. She was determined to break through all her emotional barriers of denial and shame before the day was done, whatever it took.

It took some time. Shyness and fear would arrest her free flow of movement at every attempt, it seemed. At last, Gavin, who had sat still and quiet all the while so as not to break her concentration, risked intruding.

"You're trying too hard again, Meggie. Just let it come to you," he said softly.

She knew what he meant, and she also knew that he understood. There had been no need to fear his eyes at all. She turned to face him now, and this time as soon as she began she took off like a bird. Her naked soul did not mind exposure after all, she found. It loved its vulnerability rather, and rejoiced in its freedom. She whirled and twirled pirouettes through the fragrant woodland air, her voice trilling high and light into the blue sky. Her Dance and Song were exultant, unparalleled now. She felt that she would never stop moving again.

When at last she did, Gavin adorned her with garlands of bright flowers.

"Meggie," he said, his eyes glistening, "the things I make are silly wee baubles a child would soon tire of, but what you have made today would bring tears to the eyes of a stone and sway the branches of a windless tree. It was the most beautiful thing I have ever seen!"

Meggie smiled, knowing deep inside her that what he said was true. Her fears of inadequacy were conquered forever now, and, even as she stood, she felt the old mask of competitive stubbornness, which had always hidden her in shadow just melt away into the steamy sunlight. For the first time in her life, dark, broody Meggie allowed herself to shine freely, naked and unashamed.

Chapter 19

THE SACRIFICE OF THE CORN KING

A FEW days after that, the Mootmen decided that the corn harvest should begin. It was unusually early, but the long, hot summer had ripened the crops quickly, and to leave them in the ground any longer was to risk damage from the heavy rains the Old Woman had forecast. Thunderstorms often heralded a change in the weather.

Thus the next day, after the animals were milked and everything set in order, the people of the Long Stones met by the sheltered haugh that they tilled as common cropland. They assembled first on the hillslope above to survey the rigs of corn, which curved like serpents up the contour of the haugh by the irrigation burn. It was a bonny sight. The long striped bands of cream and gold rippled gently in the breeze as if they were breathing; the lines of oats, barley, bere and rye so ripe and full that the dark furrows between them could scarcely be seen at all.

The people stood for a while in silence cherishing the scene, then Meggie, with her new-found confidence, led them all in a song. She made up the verses as she went along and sang them alone, but everyone joined in the choruses, singing them slowly and embellishing them with melismatic harmonies. It was a song of love and pride for the beautiful land they belonged to, whose produce was their life. To reap crops without first showing such appreciation would have been unthinkable.

SONG OF THE LAND

I am the land of the purple mountains
Whose grassy slopes are my gowns so rare,
The sweet meadow flowers are my precious jewels,
The long rigs of corn are my golden hair.

Through the bitter winter I lie sleeping
When the north winds from the ice-lands blow
Into the black night I go dreaming
Under my blanket of frost and snow.

I am the land of the purple mountains
Whose grassy slopes are my gowns so rare,
The sweet meadow flowers are my precious jewels,
The long rigs of corn are my golden hair.

In springtime I am the child of promise
Whose budding beauty crowns the trees,
In autumn decked in regal splendour
I bring the Sun King to his knees.

I am the land of the purple mountains
Whose grassy slopes are my gowns so rare,
The sweet meadow flowers are my precious jewels,
The long rigs of corn are my golden hair.

But under the bright blue skies of summer
I clothe myself in my finest dress:
The fruits I yield to feed my children,
I give with joy their lives to bless.

I am the land of the purple mountains
Whose grassy slopes are my gowns so rare,
The sweet meadow flowers are my precious jewels,
The long rigs of corn are my golden hair.

* * *

Song of the Land

D

The harvest went well. It took many long days of hard work to complete, but the singing and piping that accompanied it took the strain off. The best musicians were used to keep up an even rhythm, to which sickle-arms could swing for hours without tiring. They worked in teams, each new shift bringing refreshments for the one that had just finished, and praise for the amount of sheaves it had gathered.

That made for quick progress and, since the imminent rain held off, they were able to slacken off the working pace towards the end. They aimed to finish the harvest on the most auspicious day — shortly after the new moon on the eve of Lughnasadh. What could be better than to celebrate the feast of Harvest Home on the day of Lugh, the Corn King himself?

At last that day dawned, and the sun rose to find one last sheaf of corn still standing in the last rig. This was no ordinary sheaf to be stacked, winnowed and ground along with the rest, for it contained the spirit of the corn of the future rather than the bounty of the present year. Its seed was as yet only potential; it had not yet borne fruit of its own. Thus was this last sheaf called the Maiden, and it would be garnered with ritual reverence in the evening by the Corn Maiden herself.

All day long that sheaf stood in solitary vigil, drinking of the sun's golden rays for the last time, until the hour of its sacrifice drew near. The people of the Long Stones, dressed one and all in their festive finery, gathered round to witness the dramatic scene. To begin with, the Old Woman divided the sheaf into three parts, giving the first to a young boy, the second to Gavin and the third to the Elder, to hold under the ears. These three parts represented the three roles of the Corn Spirit during its life cycle — Son, Consort and Father. Meggie played the part of the Corn Maiden, in whom and for whom the Corn Spirit lived. She walked solemnly now along the length of the rig, dressed in a green cloak and leather boots. When she reached the sheaf she removed the cloak, revealing a plain brown dress under-neath, to represent the autumn earth after the corn was cut. Next she removed her boots, standing barefoot and bare-legged on the soil to show her undying connection to the Earth Mother. Finally, she picked up the ritual sickle kept only for this purpose and held it aloft in both hands. The sheaf had to be cut cleanly into its three parts, with a single stroke for each, and then must not be allowed to touch the ground. If any of these taboos were violated, the virtue could pass out of the sacred sheaf and be lost, and the prosperity of the future crop lost along with it. Everyone was depending on Meggie to perform this ritual without flaw.

She paused with held breath now, aware of the many eyes upon her. The crowd held its breath in sympathy, willing her to succeed. At last she breathed out and swooped, cutting the first part of the sheaf with a single, deft stroke, while the young boy whipped up the stalks by the ears before they could touch the ground. All was well. The crowd clapped and cheered.

When they fell silent again, Meggie turned to face Gavin. She raised her sickle to cut, but before she could move she seemed to see, in a vision, green tendrils and corn-shoots growing all over him, creeping round his forehead and spiralling upwards like two great horns from either side of his head. His lips did not move, but she heard him speak.

"I am the Corn King proud and tall," said Gavin. "Will you cut me down and kill me? Have I wronged you that you should treat me thus?"

"No, you have not wronged me, fair one," Meggie felt herself replying mentally. "I will not cut you down but will keep you forever safe with me."

The sickle seemed to grow heavy in her hands. She would lay it down and walk away with Gavin in her arms. Abruptly, Annis's voice resounded in her head.

"Corn Maiden, you cannot walk away from this task. The

99

Corn King must be sacrificed for the sake of his people. If you keep him for yourself, the rest of his people will die. Do not lay down the sickle, but cut him down now with resolve."

Meggie looked at Gavin again. He was sprouting tender green leaves from his red hair, and his pale eyes shone like a woodland creature's. He was beautiful, wild and innocent. She just could not wield the sickle.

"Cut, Meggie!" commanded Annis. "The Corn Spirit must die for his people. Would you think only of yourself and fail them?"

Meggie knew then that she had to do as Annis bid, though it would break her heart. Her eyes stinging with tears and her teeth gritted, she swung the sickle forcefully, and felt it cut right through Gavin's legs with a sickening crunch. She heard him scream and seemed to see him falling, falling, falling over a cliff-edge into the sea, never to return to her. She felt stricken: bitter and betrayed at having been left behind to mourn. She should have been the one to die for her people, not him.

The crowd, in the meantime, neither saw nor heard any of this. They only saw Meggie falter and tremble before beginning her second cut of the corn. The tension mounted in the crowd with each passing moment. Surely she would not fail them? At last, thankfully, she seemed to regain her composure enough to cut straight through the cornstalks as before. Gavin lifted them up in triumph without dropping any to the ground. There was an audible sigh of relief from the onlookers, tempered with concern for Meggie, who still seemed to be reeling under some inexplicable strain. She lunged at the third cut almost frantically, her eyes shut. Luckily the Elder was prepared. He fed the cornstalks smartly through the sickle blade for her, and held them fast. Meggie's head hung low.

The Spirit of the Corn at least was bound now, and safe. He had sacrificed himself willingly once again to bring future riches to his people. It was the way things must always be. The Old Woman, who had long learned the wisdom of accepting this, came forward to help Meggie to do the same. She scooped up some earth in her right hand and, grasping both Meggie's hands tightly in her left, she pressed the earth to the centre of the girl's forehead.

"Corn Maiden," said the old one firmly, "mourn not for the Corn King you have cut down, for he dies of his own accord. He is not lost forever, but after a season of rest returns transformed and, always, his new form is greater and grander than the one he left behind."

"Is that always so?" asked Meggie hopefully, lifting her eyes so that her unspilled tears now splashed down her cheeks openly.

"Always," said the Old Woman decisively.

Meggie turned and looked at Gavin, who was standing there winking at her, a cheeky lop-sided grin on his face as usual. She did not know whether to laugh or cry with relief as the fears of her strange vision faded. Even if it came true, how could Gavin ever be grander or greater than he was now? He was impossible, but perfect! She grinned back at him, despite herself.

Now that Meggie was smiling again, the Old Woman stepped back quietly and the ritual continued as rehearsed. The holders of the three parts of the sheaf each selected a small number of long straight stalks from their bundles and handed the rest to the three Mothers behind them. Then they each plaited their stalks into the flat intertwined loops of a Lovers' Knot which they presented to Meggie with a kiss and a blessing. The Old Woman fastened the ends of the three Knots together and pinned them to Meggie's head as a triangular golden crown.

The Mothers, meanwhile, fashioned the three bundles of corn into the form of a Maiden. The Elder's bundle became her head and body, Gavin's her arms, and the young boy's her full skirts. She was dressed in white linen and given a broom of holly twigs to carry. This Maiden would stand in the Old Woman's house for six months, guarding its precious golden seeds of promise, until Imbolc, when it would be dismantled and its cornstalks used to weave the Mother's basket that cradled the Willow-Baby. This symbolic transformation reflected the mystery of the Earth herself, who turns from Maiden to Mother miraculously each springtime, as new life bursts forth from the buried seed and the dead, decayed matter of the old season's growth.

But that is another story. For now, the Maiden was handed to Meggie, who held it before her for all to see.

"Behold the Maiden!" proclaimed the Old Woman. The company knelt in front of Meggie, and the Old Woman began to chant.

"Behold the Maiden, Mother-of-all,
Whose child is the Sun, and the corn so tall,
His golden seeds under her apron she keeps,
She brings them to ripeness, and then she them reaps.
Behold the Maiden, Mother-of-all,
Whose child is the Sun, and the corn so tall,
In the autumn she cuts him down dead to the earth,
So again in the spring she can bring him to birth.
Behold the Maiden, Mother-of-all,
Whose child is the Sun, and the corn so tall,
She gives us his body to share amongst men,
That his death on the kernstone may bring life again.
Behold the Maiden, Mother-of-all!
Behold her son, the corn so tall!"

Then the rest of the company responded:

"We hail the Maiden, Mother-of-all!
We hail her son, the corn so tall!"

That was the ceremony over. To the skirl of the pipes, Meggie and the Corn Maiden led the procession back to the Old Woman's cottage to celebrate the feast of Harvest Home.

Chapter 20

SILVER MOON AND BLUE WATER

IT was a feast that was to be remembered for many years to come for its lavish hospitality. The summer's good weather had provided an abundance of fruits, vegetables, milk, butter and cheeses, and the calm seas had yielded a more-than-generous supply of fish. Most remarkable of all, however, was Meggie's sacred Apple Tree, which had been laden with the sweetest fruits ripe for the plucking since it had rooted in February and now, in apple season, it was groaning under the weight of its crop. The whole clachan had been supplied with its fresh fruit throughout the past months and were visibly healthier for it. They now baked apples in bannocks and cakes, cooked them in the pot with their meat, and pressed them for juice. There was no end to their bounty.

Even without money, there is a certain richness in living a life of good health, free from the fear of starvation and cold. This richness is open-hearted, full-blooded and unstinting in its generosity, and such were the celebrations at the Old Woman's cottage that night.

After a few hours, though, Meggie tired of merrymaking. The image of Gavin, as Corn King, falling into the sea in sacrifice, still haunted and disturbed her even through the rollicking choruses and wild dances of the crowd. It caught her like a lump in the throat, a yearning for something that was missing in enjoyment and warm companionship. She tried to dismiss the feeling at last, but, instead of dying, it flooded through her then like a river in spate. The noise and press of the crowd became too claustrophobic to bear. Moving silently through the shadows, Meggie stepped out of the house unseen to breathe the pure night air alone.

Lost in thought, she began to walk away until the rousing strains of the revelry were but a faint echo in the darkness behind her, and towards the Moon, low-slung in the sky, she went. The Moon was the most slender crescent, and beside it shone Venus, the Evening Star. What a beautiful pair they made, Meggie mused, as her feet took her she knew not where. Curving Moon and Star so bright — like a silver sickle ready to garner a brilliant seed, or a salmon of wisdom leaping high to catch a hazelnut of inspiration falling on his sacred pool. Perhaps the Moon was a fishing-boat, sailing with its load towards the safe light of home, or perhaps — she thought with a wistfulness that caught her like a sudden pang — the Moon was a weeping eye closed against a vision of sadness and the Star a single, falling tear.

She stopped in her tracks and closed her own eyes now against unbidden, brimming tears, and, through the darkness, a lone voice reached her. It was pure and poignant as a wading-bird in the willows, and sang an ancient lament of sorrow and solitude. It was like a woman's keening for a husband lost at sea or a son killed in battle, expressing a sadness that, once felt, can never be forgotten.

The song drew Meggie softly on till, when she dared to open her eyes and discover the singer, she found herself by the seashore, at the mouth of the irrigation burn. There, at the very place where the river water spilled as an eternal sacrifice to the great ocean, sat Annis, enshrouded in a silvery, spidery cloak, washing a web of silver cloth in the water. Under her long white hair her face shone with a mysterious blue light, and her eyes were dark and deep as the sea.

She turned to Meggie saying: "My song of lament is for the dead Lord of the Corn, who was cut down this day in his prime. Will you help me escort him to the Isle of the

Blessed, where his soul may find rest and peace after his ordeal?"

"That I surely will," replied Meggie, "for it was I who brought him to his sorry fate."

"Then come," said Annis, draping over Meggie's head the silver web that she had been washing in the water.

As Annis sang again, Meggie became aware that the lament had a curious rhythm of its own. It was not even like the reaping tunes, but more tidal, rising and falling in pulses like the waves upon the shore, and the sighing of her own breath. It was like the Moon who pulls the waters and the tides of sorrow that well within.

"Reach for me," whispered the Moon through the song. "Draw me into you and let me move you."

Meggie felt the subtle urges of the Moon cascading down to her like fountains of silver through the magic of the song, and began to dance in harmony with it. As she caught sight of her limbs rippling sinuously, she realised that she too shone blue, and beneath the thin web of moonlight cloak both she and Annis were completely naked, naked and open to Moon and Water. She moved with the waves of the shore, dancing around and within their lapping, blue and silvery just like them, sharing their secrets of belonging. She was part of the one water, the ocean of life to which all of us owe our bright beginning and our blessed end. Deeper and deeper she entered it, accepting its caresses, giving her soul to its flow and changes. She could now no longer tell whether Annis was still singing or whether the water itself sang the rhythms of the dance within her. She only moved.

Annis and Meggie dived deep and deep into the great kingdom under the waves, where dazzling fish dangled and darted nimbly amid weedy forests, where anemones red and purple streamed like proud banners on castles of coral, where long tentacles slinked lithely away from unseen owners to trap unwary prey. Deeper and deeper still they dived into the dark waters of the unknown, where ugly flatfish that have never been seen, far less named, lurked sulkily in the shadows, and sea-serpents older than the earth's hills slithered in the slime that hid sunken ships wrecked on treacherous rocks. Still they plunged further, until the sucking mud engulfed them and they succumbed to oblivion. They passed passively through its black void for an age, until forcibly ejected out the other side through a narrow vortex overgrown with weeds.

They emerged eventually on to a clear sandy beach, feeling cleansed and refreshed. The drowsy liquid air around them was sweet on the lungs, the sand soft and warm underfoot. They stood upon the shore in silence, still swaying slightly from the rhythms of the deep ocean tides they had passed through. Suddenly, some maidens as naked and blue as themselves ran out from the machair and greeted them profusely, embracing them with total acceptance. Laughing, they took each other's hands and ran back through the meadowland of lush sea-plants to the coral garden of the Queen.

It was a garden of unimaginable delights, at the heart of which stood a tall throne of creamy coral, crowned with a delicate filigree fan through which tiny fish floated upon the liquid air. Upon this wonder, the Queen of the Isle of the Blessed herself sat. Her skin was as dark as the sea at midnight, but it radiated a resplendent aura of silvery-white, rippling with every pastel shade under the Moon. She was clothed in a fine web of silvery silk — so fine indeed that it was impossible to tell whether it was really cloth, or simply the sparkle of light upon the black skin, like the silvery sheen of moonlight on water. Her long hair flowed greeny like a fern over her shoulders from combs of coral, and round her neck and arms hung circlets of pearls, heavy and sweet with the scent of jasmine.

Meggie automatically fell to her knees at the exquisite splendour of this being. "All hail to thee, Queen Mara Undersea," she said reverently. "Thy beauty and honour are unsurpassed."

"On the contrary," replied the Queen, lifting Meggie up and kneeling before her instead. "It is you I hail, O Queen of the harvest. Well sits thy crown of gold upon thy head. I am blessed and humbled by thy presence here."

Meggie was taken aback by this reversal. What crown of gold was the Queen referring to? She put her hands to her head and discovered with surprise that she was still wearing the little headdress of Lovers' Knots that the Old Woman had pinned there so long before at the ceremony of the reaping. She was puzzled. The crown was no fine thing at all, for it was made only of old cornstalks. Why should the Queen admire it so?

In answer, the Queen held up her hands, with the palms facing. Between them a web of silver suddenly spun and shimmered, then settled into a misty film of blue. Meggie looked into it and saw, as in a mirror, her face reflected. This was no ordinary mirror, however, for it showed things reflected as they truly are, and not as they appear to be. Meggie explored her face as if it were that of a stranger, staring deeply into the dark eyes of untold mystery. She saw her hair flowing and shining in the liquid air around her, and, upon her head, the crown of gold. Now she understood. The cornstalks were not withered and dead as she remembered them, but glistened from within with the golden light of the Sun. She saw that this Sun-light was the most valuable treasure she could have brought, for the Land-under-the-Sea has no Sun in its cloudscape and, for all its natural beauty, it has no corn either, which is the earthly complement of the Sun's life-giving essence. This was why the Mara knelt before her in veneration — she, Meggie, was crowned with the light of the Lord of Life himself, while the Queen Undersea could claim no such title.

Now that she understood why her own position as Corn Maiden and Harvest Queen was so sacred and so exalted, Meggie knew that there was only one thing to do. She took the corn-gold crown from her own head and placed it on that of the kneeling sea-Queen, saying: "On thee I bestow the honour that was given me, O Queen. I willingly give to thee the Sun of my own life, in adoration."

The Mara rose smiling. "Well hast thou passed the test, my child. For to sacrifice one's life and one's high standing is more noble a thing in my realm than to claim title. Even the Lord of the Corn himself becomes truly great only when he is cut down. So it is not for me to claim the golden crown for myself, lest my throne be forfeit to one who surpasses me in humility and bounty. But within the crown lies the soul of the King you have brought to me. For six months would he rest within my realm to be refreshed after his sojourn on the earth's bleak surface. Then, for six months, would he valiantly return to the world of men, that they might be nourished by his beneficence. So now let us both choose to release his soul from our bondage, and thus ourselves be redeemed."

Fingertip to fingertip they lifted the fragile crown from the Mara's head and together laid it gently down upon the coral sands. The kernels of life in the three Lovers' Knots each burst forth then in full glory, sprouting into fine golden horses with silvery, silken manes and tails. They whinnied in delight at their new-found freedom, then capered and cantered away into the meadowlands beyond to browse upon the lush sea-grasses.

Meggie was overcome with pleasure at the beauty and exhilaration of the transformed Corn King. She remembered that the Old Woman had said that the new form is always grander than the old, and now she had seen for herself that it was so. It was the way things must always be. Such sacrifice, freely chosen, was clearly more than its own reward, and she saw that there was no need at all to mourn for those who undertook it.

Freed now from her reaping-burden of grief and guilt, Meggie joined Annis, the Mara, and the many other blue maidens in a feast of songs and dances, basking in the dreamy delights of the Isle of the Blessed, until time — that unrelenting taskmaster — called her home again. Mara embraced her warmly before she left and presented her with a large, curving shell of glimmering mother-of-pearl, telling her that if she blew a note upon it, the undines of the water would come to her in attendance.

Meggie put the shell to her lips. The note that she blew was full of the haunting sadness of the sea, like the cry of the gull and the call of the seal. It was a note full of the yearning of men to leave their loved ones and cross the ocean, and like a siren it could lure a sailor to his death beneath the waves. And yet, that sad and haunting note of death was pregnant with life: full of the undertones of all the species of living creatures that ever once welled from the water's depths. It told of their birth and growth, and then of their suffering and sacrifice. It was a note almost too powerful for the human soul to bear.

As its reverberations faded away, Meggie realised that she was swaying helplessly in the hazy blue of its mesmeric echo. The feeling was rapturous, but also somehow dangerous. She knew instinctively that she should never sound that note again unless the situation was of the gravest: a matter of life and death itself.

She felt the Mara cradle her then in her soothing, silvery aura of wisdom and peace, and lay her in the mother-of-pearl shell. It drifted like a dream to the surface of the water, and washed her ashore on the white-shelled beach of home.

Chapter 21

HAIL AND FAREWELL

MEGGIE stepped out on to solid ground, revelling in the sharp crunch of shells underfoot and the smell of early autumn in the landwind. The Isle of the Blessed was a charming place without a doubt, she thought, but it was not home.

She turned back to the sea-shallows to pick up the Mara's gift. The mother-of-pearl shell, which had borne her safely back on the journey from beneath the bed of the ocean, was small enough to fit into her cupped hands. She examined it carefully, wondering at its magic.

"Nothing is impossible," she mused, "if such marvels as this are but a dream away. Rock, wave, tree, shell — all simple things tell of the mysteries of creation if we but know how to listen and feel. Some think they must journey to the ends of the earth to find the answers to their questions, but all secrets are whispered on the very air around us, and our home ground provides our every need. . . "

Her peaceful reflections were disturbed then by Annis laying a hand on her shoulder. A long silent look of understanding passed between them.

"Well, my soul," said Annis at last, "my true friend and my equal, the time has come when I must say unto you: hail and farewell."

Meggie's calm eyes became as troubled as a windswept lake. "What do you mean, hail and farewell? Will you not come for me again to journey at Samhain? I have so much to learn from you, and I am only just beginning to understand what you have shown me. You surely cannot mean farewell!" she burst out.

Annis waited a long time before replying, searching deep into Meggie's eyes. She saw there the unquenchable yearning of a soul that had been quickened with the soft touch of light and love, but had not yet been stretched in challenge or blossomed into maturity. She saw that Meggie did not know the true value of the tokens of the four Elements that she had gained from the Sidhe queens. She was obviously not aware that the four tokens were something few achieved in a whole lifetime's painful striving, never mind in one short year of pleasure. She saw that Meggie did not feel any proud satisfaction at her fine achievement, with which she could return to the world to bless, teach and heal as a Wise Woman marked with distinction. She saw instead that Meggie still felt young, inexperienced and helpless within, her soul full of unconscious aspirations and unformed questions. She knew that for a soul such as this — a rare one indeed — there would be no contentment in returning to the earth with a position of honour. This one would not come up to her own expectations or grant her yearning soul rest until she had penetrated the heart of the Mystery of Life and Death itself, and understood the deepest Secrets of Creation. And with that Annis could not help her.

Sadly she replied, knowing what fate must lie before so rare a one as this: "I can come to you no more, my soul-light, for there is no more that I can teach you. You already know more than I, and your innocence shames my inadequacy."

She held up her hand to stem the inevitable storm of protest she knew would come tumbling from the lips of the now-bewildered Meggie.

"Believe me, my child, you are well blessed by the Nameless One within, and know as much as you need of her ways to become in turn to another as I am to you. But if you would know more before you turn your eyes back to the world without, there is but one teacher who can aid you. I cannot tell you her name, but you will see her face in the Well at the World's End. It is the face of the Goddess herself."

Meggie stood numb for a while absorbing this. Then she replied: "But surely you would come with me on such a journey, guiding me with your kind wisdom as you have done before."

"Alas I cannot, for this journey must be undertaken alone."

"Then I have not the skill to succeed. It is only with your help that I was able to journey and return before."

Annis replied, "If you but knew it, my love, it was not my skill but yours alone that led you safely on the journeys you have taken. For each creates the worlds that they will face in the Kingdoms of the Elements by their own hopes and fears. It was your purity of heart, and not my wisdom, that brought you with grace and dignity through each of these experiences. But now the sun is rising and it is time for us to part."

With that, Annis quickly turned and disappeared into the dark western water before Meggie could see the sadness welling in her heart. Meggie did not need to see: the air around was heavy and wet with it. With her shell clutched tight, she made her way through the dewy grass to the sheiling.

* * *

Rain fell ceaselessly for days. Meggie watched it through the tiny window of the hillside hut, lashing down and blurring the reality of the outside world. The few times she ventured outside, biting autumn winds whipped her face. The soft fragrant breezes of spring and summer were gone forever.

Meggie's mood was as desolate as the weather. She felt that her childhood and her innocent happiness had been cruelly torn away like still-green leaves ripped from their boughs by storm-winds. She tried hard to evoke pleasant memories of the journeys she had taken with Annis, and, briefly, she could recall fleeting feelings of bliss and serenity, wonder and acceptance. But, always, these gentle visions would be destroyed by the overwhelming bleakness of the last memory: the final parting with Annis by the shores of the sea.

She thought that she understood why she had to feel this way. The lesson of Lughnasadh was that of sacrifice — the giving up of what you hold most dear for redemption. Yearly, the Corn King gave his very life for the salvation of his people, and chose to do so freely and bravely. Now she had been asked to give up her magical journeys with Annis.

It was the tiniest strand of her life, and only one small aspect of love. How mean and miserable she felt her soul to be that she resented giving up even this. She had probably had no true claim to this wonderful experience in the first place. It had come to her unbidden after all, and may not have been hers by birthright. The gods give and the gods take away. Everything occurred as it should in its own time and tide with a harmony and measure that defied human understanding. She knew well enough that there was no point in railing against the decrees of the gods. One could only admit and absorb the experience given, whatever its nature, for all was part of the endless cycles of the one life. Death inevitably followed birth, and the agony of loss inevitably followed the ecstasy of love. She turned all this over and over in her mind, looking at it from every angle she could. She tried hard to accept and understand her fate with the dignity of the Old Woman, but try as she might she could not. No amount of reasoning could calm the stormy seas of sorrow within her, for she felt that her own failings must be to blame for Annis's departure.

The other maidens at the sheiling, seeing her pale, love-lorn face staring blankly through the rainy window day after day, began to avoid her and talk of her in low whispers.

They said that she must be elf-struck: that she had been shot by a faery bolt and had an invisible wound through which her life-essence was draining away into the faery realms, never to return. Meggie heard their whisperings and felt their fears, but she made no attempts to reassure them for she knew that in some way they were right. She did indeed feel incurably wounded and that her heart and soul were irretrievably lost to the Otherworlds. The worry and suffering she was causing her friends only added to her burden, however, and as the days went on she felt more and more wretched, until at last she had to leave. Without a word of explanation, she walked out of the world of the maidens and went to stay in the quiet sanctuary of the Old Woman's cottage.

The Old Woman proved a more sympathetic companion. She listened with interest to Meggie's stories of her journeys, and told the young girl of her own experiences with the fair folk. She explained that there was often no cure for the sweet sorrow of longing for them, save that it would turn to healing wisdom as time went by.

In the meantime, she did all that she could to alleviate the girl's affliction. She prepared fragrant brews of invigorating herbs sweetened with honey to give her back the vitality of a bee a-busying. She bade her wear her petticoat wrong side out, to banish the influences of life-sapping shades. And every night, when she tucked the girl up in red woollen blankets by the fireside, she heated the iron poker red-hot in the flames and drew a protective circle with it round the bed. All these things and more she did for her beloved Meggie, but to no avail. As she had suspected, the source of Meggie's sadness was deeper and stronger than the magic of the cures.

For all that, Meggie enjoyed her stay and proved to be good company. She shared the Old Woman's love of herbs and together they ground, bottled and labelled the summer's dried bunches, and prepared unguents, lotions, potions and wines for every conceivable ague and ill. Meggie was especially fascinated with the carved kist of spices and resins from across the far seas. Sometimes the Old Woman would let her break the wax seal on one of the pottery jars in it and release the exotic, powdery fragrance into the room. At other times she would simply hold a sealed jar in her hands and sit quietly with her eyes shut, until pictures formed in her mind of the foreign land from which it had come.

The clearest pictures always came with rosemary, the herb of remembrance. She would see a village of white houses clustered round paved streets shimmering with heat, sloping down to an intensely bright, azure blue sea. After a while, if she persisted, she could even hear goats bleating, pigs grunting, and children's chants and laughter. She held the rosemary jar at night one time and saw four men walking with lamps down to the shore, singing a song with modal harmonies quite unlike her own. Although she could not understand the words, she knew it was a song of adoration to the Lady Moon. The men rowed out to sea in a fishing-boat, still humming their chorus. Their Moon was large and bright on the horizon, just like hers outside, but Meggie was amazed to see that it was not white, but deep red in colour. Truly there were more wonders in the world than she had ever dreamed of.

Sometimes she would go out walking at twilight, when few other people were abroad. If she half-closed her eyes, she found that she could see the long, lithe bodies of the sylphs gliding on the breezes, and down by the sea she could discern little merfolk riding on the waves. All around the meadowland elfin lights danced for her, and the fair-faced dryad of her own Apple Tree tinkled in greeting whenever she approached. The whole landscape was alive with Faery just for her. It should have made her happy that she could see the Otherworld in her own country, but somehow it just seemed to make her nostalgia for the realms that were lost to her even more acute.

Apart from the Old Woman, the only other person

Meggie cared to see now was Gavin. When the others had shunned her up at the sheiling, he had come up to her hut every evening through the driving rain to comfort her. He had sat with her in silence, holding her hands and sharing her sorrow. He had not judged her like the girls, nor had he fussed and worried like the women. He had not even tried to cure her. He had simply been there with her, and that was enough.

Although he did not require it, Meggie had tried to find some way to express her loving gratitude for his devotion. Up at the sheiling she had tried to force herself out of her depression and speak to him, but that had only made things worse. The words would stick in her throat, coming out like ugly sobs. Now, at the Old Woman's cottage, she found a better way. When Gavin came round of an evening, instead of going out to him, she would turn herself further inwards, probing deep into her sense of anomie, and sinking into its pain until it welled through her. Sometimes it would express itself in dance, sometimes in song, and, at other times, poetry of great beauty that she had not composed would be recited through her lips.

There were different qualities to her creations depending, perhaps, on which way the wind blew. Sometimes they would be dark and lusty as the Earth; sometimes light and sweet as the Air; sometimes sharp and quick as Fire; other times cool and blue as Water. Yet, always, they had a graceful perfection that was out of this world and quite entrancing.

So the weeks went by, Meggie becoming more and more introspective until her dreaming and her reality were well nigh one and the same. At last the eve of Samhain arrived once again, cloudy and grey as ever. As the day wore on, Meggie became increasingly aware of the tides of change that blurred the boundaries between this world and the next. She grew restless and ached for relief from the overwhelming pull, but feared to cross the threshold and face the hosts of wandering spirits that would taunt and then leave her. As the sun began to sink, however, she could resist it no longer and ran outside. To the north of the glen something was forming for her out of the mists. It was a bridge.

Now she understood! What she had to sacrifice was not what she had thought, but something greater still, that was so precious and so close to her that she had not even considered it. Yet now that it was demanded of her, it was easy to let go.

She went back inside and fetched her yewen plate and mother-of-pearl shell from under her pillow, and a blossoming spray of her Apple Tree from the jug on the dresser. She put everything into the green woollen bag and slung it over her shoulder, then wrapped herself in her warmest shawl and cloak. The Old Woman was dozing by the fireside. It was better so, Meggie thought. She planted a kiss on the grey head, whispered her thanks, and left.

The bridge was waiting for her. She walked upon its misty path, up through the Long Stones and on to the Moothill. At the top she turned and looked behind her at the land where she had lived all her life. She could not see much through the dusky gloom, but in her mind's eye it was as clear as noon. There were the glens, the low cottages, the haughs, the sheilings. There were the heather slopes, the woods and her favourite Apple Tree. There were the burns going through the machair to the white-shelled beach. She loved it all.

"Hail and farewell," she called to it, raising her hand in salute. She was sure that it answered her, even though she heard nothing. She turned now to climb down the northern slope of the Moothill and disappeared into a thick wall of mist.

Chapter 22

THE CALLING-SPELL

WHEN the Old Woman awoke a short time later, she knew that Meggie had gone. She also knew, without looking, what things the girl had taken with her. It came as no real surprise. Out of the window she could see the mists of Samhain eddying and swirling from the north. They were thicker than usual, as if to hide some secret. The Old Woman sighed heavily. It did not bode well.

Deep within her heart of hearts the Old Woman had always known that the pattern of Meggie's life contained a strange spiral which she could not fathom. She had seen it in birdflight and leaf-fall on the day the girl had been born. It would not reveal its origin or its conclusion to her, but it demanded acknowledgement nevertheless.

"As the girl grows, guide her as the Moon does," she had counselled her mother. "Seek not to make of her what you will, but draw out of her what she already is inside." The advice had been inadequate perhaps, but the best she could give at the time.

Through the years the Old Woman had watched the girl grow through light moods and dark. When as a young child she had gone to the shady woods alone to dance and sing in secret, the Old Woman had seen it with the clear sight of her mind's eye. She had also noticed the effect that her movements and sounds had on nature: plants seemed to visibly grow around her, and wild creatures frisk and nuzzle their fellows in delight. It was an uncommon ability she had without a doubt, the more so because Meggie herself seemed totally unaware that she possessed it.

This last year the Old Woman had watched Meggie's gift gradually begin to surface from the darkness of the unconscious into the light of day. The whole fabric of life in the clachan had been uplifted and blessed by it. In particular, its magic had transformed Gavin from an awkward, stammering lad into a confident, accomplished young man.

The Old Woman had watched these developments with pleasure and satisfaction. Soon, she had felt, the time would be right to instruct the girl in the ancient arts of Power and Making. Then, when the day came when her own weary body was laid to rest and her soul set free, there would be one left behind on the surface of the earth to become in time Old Woman to the tribe.

That was how things should have gone. Meggie showed outstanding promise as a future Wise Woman, but needed many years of experience to learn how to accept and wield her natural talents properly. It was not right that she should have been taken from the world while still unfledged. Now she would feel abandoned and comfortless in the Otherworld, and her people would be left bereft of her wisdom.

The Old Woman frowned. What could have caused such a premature summoning for the little one? She could think of only one thing: that the girl had rashly made some extravagant oath under circumstances that demanded its fulfilment. Ah, the impetuosity of youth! Only with age came the good sense to see all and say nothing. The Old Woman sighed deeply for the second time.

It was a tricky situation to remedy. If the girl had made an oath in the hearing of the Sidhe, there was nothing the Old Woman could do to cancel its effect, for the essence of it was already woven into the stuff of creation and had become part of the inalterable future. Indeed, to try to meddle at this stage would only further entangle the web of intrigue that Meggie had snarled in the first place.

Then what could be done for her? Since it was against the inner law to interfere with another's free will, she could not call Meggie home directly, for the girl had — albeit unwittingly — chosen to go. On the other hand, since she had failed to instruct Meggie soon enough in the ancient arts, it may be that the girl would be held in the Otherworld beyond need and against her volition, lacking the knowledge to change her shape and enter time again. On these grounds, the Old Woman felt, it was legitimate to intervene. She sighed heavily for the third time that evening, for the foolish people who envied her powers of deep understanding. They could not imagine how burdensome and difficult life could be if you possessed them.

Now that she had made up her mind to act, she moved swiftly. Water was poured from the pitcher into a shallow wooden bowl, and rock salt spooned into a shell. Charcoal was heated over the fire until it crackled and sparked, then placed in a bronze quaich. Pinches of spice and scented gums were chosen and mixed instinctively. All was ready to begin.

She held her hands first over the salt and water, saying: "Blessed be, O creature of salt, for thou art of our Mother's body. Blessed be, O creature of water, for thou art of the blood that flows in her veins."

She tipped the salt into the water and watched it dissolve. "Together you are part of the one life. From the past, you bind and seal all creatures in their fate."

She turned now to the glowing charcoal and the aromatic mixture. "Blessed be, O creature of fire, for thou art of the eye of our Father. Blessed be, O creature of incense, for thou art of his breath."

She sprinkled the incense carefully over the charcoal. Its smoke smelt acrid and somehow distant. Meggie must be far from home by now. There was no time to lose. "Together," she said to the charcoal and spices, "you stand and strive. From the unhewn rocks of fate you carve bright jewels for the future."

With bowl and quaich in hand, she went outside to walk the sunwise circle of the house. Once she circled for protection against the harbingers of chaos. Twice she circled to show the nature of her purpose. Thrice she circled to summon the attention of the elemental guardians.

The air became quiet and watchful. Even the twilight mists stopped swirling as if frozen in time. The Old Woman intoned her calling-spell to the four quarters and beyond, knowing that on this night of nights many strange ears would be listening.

> "To the dark and silent Earth I call,
> To the still and rushing Air I call,
> To the lambent, burning Fire I call,
> And to deep and gushing Water.
>
> To the white and gentle Moon I call,
> To the bright and ardent Sun I call,
> To the singing Stars of night I call,
> To ask of my love-daughter.
>
> For if my Meggie you do keep,
> If in your kingdom she does sleep,
> And if you one day hear her weep,
> Remember that I sought her.
>
> And let her then come home again,
> To her cottage, Apple Tree and glen,
> In the simple world of mortal men,
> Unbind the oath that caught her!"

She felt the reverberations of her intent travel out to the far spheres and fade away. It was done. The mists began to swirl again.

Now it would be best to let the whole affair go from her mind, and let it resolve itself in its own time and in its own uncanny way. The responsibility for this, at least, was out of her hands.

She left the bowl and quaich on the ground as an offering to the peaceful night-spirits who had attended her call, then fetched her cloak, staff and lamp. She must hurry now, before darkness fell completely, to join the assembly of Samhain at the Elder's cottage, for to her fell the duty of electing the Circle for the coming year.

Chapter 23

GAVIN'S SACRIFICE

IF the Old Woman could calmly accept Meggie's dis-
appearance from her life, Gavin could not. He was well
aware that she had gone somewhere beyond his reach and
beyond his ken — somewhere that could be dangerous to
seek wilfully — but that did not deter him. At his insistence,
he and the Old Woman scried for a sign of what had befallen
her. They looked at pictures in the firelight and in the
clouds. They looked at images in the mirror surface of water
in a soot-blackened bowl. They cast sticks upon the ground
and read their shapes. Many things they saw, but of Meggie
there was no trace at all. It was as if she had simply disappeared off the face of the earth and had left no footsteps
behind her. At last the Old Woman gave him stern warning
to forget her and return to his tasks.

Gavin was distraught. Even if he had seen her dead, it would
have been better than this empty silence. It echoed inside him
like the sound of a stone dropping in a bottomless well.
Whatever the Old Woman might say, he could never abandon
Meggie.

At night he began to dream recurrently of a beautiful
maiden dancing and singing with all the charm of a summer's
day. He would run towards her shouting "Meggie, wait!", but
the faster he ran the further away she seemed to be. When at
last he stood upon her shadow and so held her fast, she would
turn to him with arms outstretched, calling him on. He would
reach for her and fall over a clifftop into the sea, drowning in
the treacherous waters of his own fears.

Night after night he woke shaking from this vision, until, reluctantly, he confessed it to the Old Woman. She interpreted the dream with the cryptic ambiguity that deep truth always has.

"If you choose, or if you do not, you will seek for her endlessly, and though you will often touch her face, you will never reach her, for you will never believe in your power to do so. Ever further will you have to go, until you walk on paths that no other has trodden before you, and yet even as a child she walked further along them than you will ever go. What was her path that you must follow if you dare? For her it was as easy as a gentle slope to walk on, but for you it will be like pushing back the relentless tides of the sea that would drown you. You will never know rest or peace again."

Gavin did not understand the Old Woman's words, but after that the dream never returned. He toyed briefly with the idea of going to seek for Meggie, but knew it would be a hopeless task, and also a selfish one. The mourning of the clachan for one lost soul was bad enough; he would not have them grieve over his loss as well. The Old Woman was right. He should return to his tasks.

To take his mind from brooding, he began to look for new materials to carve and learn from. By and by, at the edge of the wood and the water, his eye chanced upon a clump of tall umbellifers, dried and dead now, but not yet decayed. He cut some lengths between nodules on the straight stalks. They were hollow inside and did not seem to offer much scope for carving. Nevertheless, he took them home with his bundle of fallen branches and laid them aside for future use.

It was not long before he was drawn to them again, his fingers itching to work with them. He still did not know what they would be good for until, after handling them for some time, he discovered that they made musical sounds when he blew over the top of them. Different lengths made different notes, so he cut a number of them to varying sizes experimentally and played a scale.

The tuning was strange: not wrong exactly, but foreign-sounding, and their tone was breathy and enigmatic. He had heard that scale and that tonal quality before somewhere. Meggie had used it when singing songs of the eastern Air. He bound the reeds together with thin twine, played the scale again, and then tried a tune. He was no musician, but even with these first efforts he could hear again the faintest echo of Meggie's music. It was enough to ensnare him.

* * *

For the next while he spent all his spare time practising on his reed pipes. He also asked the Old Woman for the little harp that Meggie had played when she had returned from the Hollow Hill, and practised on that too.

He cast aside all his other proud accomplishments and fine talents now in a secret obsession to capture the elusive sounds and wisps of half-forgotten tunes that he could still hear Meggie sing and dance in his dreams. Unfortunately, the more he tried, the more dissatisfied he became with his achievements. To him they were like crude carvings that bore a rough likeness to the original, but had none of its life or grace. He was driven wild with frustration in his attempts, but that only made him more determined to succeed in the end, whatever the price.

Next he tried improving the quality of his instruments. He made wooden pipes to replace the worn-out umbellifer stalks, experimenting long and hard with different types, lengths and thicknesses before he was content with the tonal range at his disposal. He also tried placing the finger-holes at varying intervals to give different modal scales. Some worked, and some did not. He kept the best and practised now with them.

Building a good harp was more difficult still. It needed choice timbers, seasoned to perfection and strong enough to withstand the tension of the strings. Because it took about withstand the tension of the springs. Because it took about two years for the resonance to mature, he built several to different specifications and played them all until he was familiar with their various characteristics. Finally, he chose one which had developed an especially sweet tone and named it 'Meggie's Heart', which was the sweetest thing he could think of. He carefully carved its wooden frame with intertwined serpentine patterns, reminiscent of the magical melodies and movements of his beloved one, and from then on played no other harp but this. It was by far his favourite instrument.

After that, all his energies were devoted to perfecting his music, dedicated to the memory of Meggie. No effort was too much, because it was the only thing that mattered to him any more. Although with the passing of time he found that his visions of her faded somewhat, so that he could no longer hear her voice or see her dance with any clarity in his mind, she was not lost to him. By that time he had discovered her anew in nature, where she had always belonged.

He heard her bright songs in the piping of small birds at daybreak, and the inscrutable mystique of her chants in the call of a lone owl under the moon. In the sleek streamlining of a soaring eagle or a swan alighting on water he recognised the smooth fluidity of her singing, and in the silver rainbows of a river-trout's scales, the expressive range of her voice. Tirelessly, he endeavoured to capture these qualities on his wooden pipes, always seeking new half-notes, slurs and trills to express the subtleties that he loved so much.

Mastering the pipes was not easy, but for him the harp was more difficult still, for on it he tried to express every facet of Meggie's fey beauty. In the undulation of waves upon the shore or rigs of corn in the wind he saw the elegance of her dancing limbs, and these he rendered in long rippling rolls of notes. He saw her poise in the roe deer, her deep, sad trust in the eyes of a seal, the softness of her skin in the green moss of the woodland, her dark hair upon a blackbird's back. Each delicate image of nature that caught his eye reminded him of his Meggie, and each he wove with love into his harping and into the lyrical poems that he sang with it.

Seven years later, when he was twenty-one, he left the clachan for the first time, not by way of the sea, but by the long, hard land-route to the north through the hills. He saw the new landscape around him with the keen wonder of a stranger, and its endless, awesome beauty, which was his bed and his feasting table, inspired him to still greater heights of creativity. Everywhere he looked, the ethereal vision of Meggie danced before him, elusive as a butterfly, enticing him further into the unknown and mocking him with the uncapturable sweetness of her song.

Whenever he came upon a village or community he would sing and play in return for food. He never thought to ask for a higher reward and would not accept any if offered, for his music seemed to him always flawed and worth little. In fact — though he never stayed in one place long enough to find out for himself — his art was most highly esteemed. Its fame spread far and wide, and set a new standard for bardship. His exotic trills, scales and cadences and exquisite nature lyrics influenced every aspiring musician in the land from that time forth.

Although he did not know it or believe it, Gavin was a master musician for, just as he had accepted the gift of the faery plate that Meggie had discarded that fateful night so long ago, so he had inherited the gift of her arts when she left the world behind. In truth, Poetry, Song, Music and Dance — these things that can weave magic as powerful as any wizard's spell — are the real gifts to humankind from the Sidhe of the Far Places beyond the surface of the earth. And although Gavin never saw or talked to the Sidhe folk as Meggie had done, he knew intimately both their intense joy and their intense sadness, and shared the sweet anguish of their exile from the security of domesticity.

He died at last an old man one wild Samhain night, far from the white-shelled beach and the glens rising up to the Moothill that had once been his home. The inhabitants of the northern strath where he died loved him as one of their own, but out of respect for his strange wildness they buried him not in the peaceful shelter of the glen where their own dead lay, but atop the highest mountain itself where he would always be free to wander to the four quarters and back again. Upon his cairn they planted an apple tree in memory of his charming song which began:

> A wondrous tree grows at the door of my beloved.
> It is an apple with silvery blossoms rare.
> Its fruit blushes like her soft cheeks in sunlight,
> And it calls her name on the four winds
> To bring her gently home.

As the apple tree grew, a yew tree grew alongside it, though, curious to relate, the yew was not known to flourish at all in those parts. The branches of the two trees entwined in each other like the arms of lovers as they grew, and eventually even the two trunks merged into one.

The name of Gavin the Harper became a legend more famous as the years went on. Some said he must surely have been one of the Sidhe folk on account of his red hair and pale eyes, and that his soul must have grown into that uncanny twin tree through his own enchantment. The mountain became known as the Hill of the Faery of Sweet Music, and for many generations after young harpers and pipers would visit it to ask of the tree some of its magic for their own music. Thus did the influence of Gavin the Harper live on, so that even now the Celtic poet uses the simple images of nature to describe his darling, and his most modest tunes still have the power to bring tears to the eyes of a stone and sway the branches of a windless tree.

Part Five

Beyond the Northern Wind

Chapter 24

BARROWBANE

THE mists had thinned — who knows how long ago — on to a dark, starless night that would not give way to dawn. The gibbous moon still hung heavy and bloated in the sky, appearing and disappearing fitfully behind ragged strips of black cloud. It was a dull yellow colour, affording little illumination and less comfort. Meggie staggered ever onwards under its niggardly eye, with no one to turn to for direction save the pointing fingers of the bare, straggly trees and the howling winds in the mountains.

There were no familiar landmarks that she could follow. She might be going anywhere — or nowhere. Into the darkness she was compelled to journey, but darkness, like light, pervades time and space and has no fixed stronghold. It seemed to her a journey without end.

The void of silence was at last broken by the sinister cry of a night-raven, perched like a sentinel in the tree upon her path. He flew at her so close she could feel the wind of his beating wings chilling her face. He would not let her pass.

Rather than battle with him, Meggie turned off to the left, stumbling blindly up a shadowy slope. Abruptly it levelled, and there before her was a long, low mound of rocks glimmering faintly with a spectral light. It was a burial mound for an ancient race long gone from the surface of the earth. Barrowbane was its name.

At one time the mere whisper of that name would have brought a blooded warrior quaking to his knees in terror, but Meggie had lived in enlightened, loving times and knew nothing of its reputation. Meeting its cold gaze fearlessly with her own, she decided that she would try to enter it, and leave the endless night behind.

She circled it warily, peering closely at the rubble walls, and eventually came to a halt at the narrow end where she had begun. There had been no sign of any doorway or crack. Under other circumstances she would have realised the folly of trying to break the seal on this chamber. The yellow moon, the call of the night-raven, and the fact that she had — against all her native instincts — circled it against the way of the sun, were all omens of ill. But there was nothing in this place to measure folly or wisdom by. There was only action or inaction.

Meggie took the yewen plate from her bag and pressed it against the wall of the mound.

"By all the powers of the Earth, named and nameless, I charge this wall to open here and now and admit me into the chamber."

She was surprised at the compelling power in her voice. The night-raven fluttered and skreiched over her in alarm. Meggie held fast, that her will would be done.

The green lines on the yewen plate began to throb and glow. Energy tingled from them through Meggie's body, then flashes of green darted along the mound, gathering again at the narrow end. There was a grating sound of stone on stone, and the light gradually faded.

As Meggie withdrew the plate, the black hole under it yawned into a gaping chasm, blasting her with a musty smell of dank earth and death.

"I am your destiny," it seemed to say. "You cannot escape me."

Meggie entered the chamber as if in trance, and the black hole immediately closed behind her, as solid as before. The barrow walls had been sealed irrevocably in ancient times, with powerful runes of a system of sorcery now lost to knowledge. Meggie may have entered, but she could never leave. The archaic darkness had trapped another victim in its lair. Now there was no room for regret, or for the solace of tears. There would be no second chance, no reconciliation, no improvement. There was only the certainty of death, and even that was not offered freely.

Meggie pressed on into the rank-smelling belly of the chamber, where the bones of the long-dead lay clinging to miserable shreds of old memories. They clicked and rattled disapprovingly as she disturbed them, and at first she cowered in fright.

"Go back!" they spat in contempt. "There is no place for you here."

"I cannot and I will not," said Meggie, her voice defiant, but the rest of her quivering.

"We will not let you stay. This is our domain, and we will not share it." All the bones seemed to rise on end, shaking and clattering threateningly in a chorus of "Ours, ours, ours, ours . . ." until Meggie thought her ears would burst.

"Stop!" she screamed at last, jumping up boldly and shooting out her arms. "You have no power and no essence of life. Return to the dust of the earth under my feet where you belong!"

The bones fell to the ground and lay obediently still, but morose. The intruder had won the first battle, but would lose the war.

Meggie waited to see if they would attack again, but they neither moved nor spoke. She could sense them sulking and skulking, but did not let it bother her.

"Very well," she said. "You have come to your senses. I will be on my way now. I have no wish to share your company a moment longer."

She walked on with as much dignity of bearing as her trembling legs would allow, feeling the ill-wishing eyes of the bones upon her from every side. If she could only reach the next doorway without collapsing, she felt, her ordeal would be over.

The doorway was a black hole in the far wall of the barrow. Perhaps Meggie hoped that it would lead outside again, back to the monotonous starless night. It was a pity that she had no right to hope. She got to it at last, but realised with horror that the atmosphere that lay beyond it was even blacker and more oppressive than before. Nothing on earth could induce her to cross the threshold, but equally she dared not turn back and face the derision of the bones. What could she do?

Not through mercy, she was spared the agony of decision. A bone whistled through the air behind her as if hurled by some unseen enemy and cracked her on the back of the skull. Meggie fell forward through the doorway and down a long, vertical shaft. Her head thumped on rock at the bottom, and she lost consciousness.

* * *

Meggie opened her eyes onto blackness, shut them, then opened them again. It made no difference. She could see nothing. She knew she was not dead because her every limb ached and she could taste blood in her mouth from her cut head. Something heavy seemed to be sitting on her forehead. She tentatively felt with her hand. There was nothing there but pain.

Slowly she got up and felt the walls to get her bearings. Above her, the shaft rose smooth and slippery to beyond her reach. It would be impossible to climb. As far as she could make out, she was in a circular chamber of solid rock like a cave. It took a long while to find the next doorway. It was a narrow tunnel near the floor on the far side, sloping downwards. She had no choice. If she did not want to stay here to die, she would have to brave it.

Progress was laborious and woefully slow. The further she went, the heavier her body seemed to become, until she could barely walk. The tunnel became narrower and lower

too. She was eventually reduced to crawling. All the while —
although she would not have thought it possible — the
atmosphere became blacker and blacker, the air thicker and
coarser so that it rasped her throat and lungs as she
breathed. It was bristling with animosity.

At length her mind, which had been absorbed with the
immense effort of moving her body step after step, became
aware that the atmosphere was alive and sentient. It was
composed of many beings so compressed in the darkness
that they had barely any individuality left. She stopped
briefly to assess the situation. That was a mistake. At once
they seemed to close in on her through the gloom, willing
her to fail and perish — willing her to become, like them, a
shadow of the Inner Earth.

It was nearly impossible to oppose them. Her strength
was failing, and she felt that she was suffocating, but she
resisted as best she could. To keep herself from hearing
their suggestions that she lay down and die, she focused her
mind on her pain. It made her movements even more
burdensome, but at least she still moved.

Her efforts were valiant but doomed. At last the air before
her became so intensely black with ill will that it felt solid.
She could not go on. Her last dregs of vitality seemed to
drain away into it. It was the end. She lay down under the
great burden of oppression, flattened against the rock floor.
It was icy cold beneath her.

There was one warm spot to her right side. Inch by inch,
her hand crept up towards it. Whatever it was, it was her only
chance. Her fingers closed round the yewen plate. Living
energy pulsed down her arm and through her body. She
could make it now. She flipped up suddenly, holding the
plate before her like a shield.

"Begone!" she commanded the darkness. "Let me go
free."

Green light flashed from the plate like sword thrusts. The
shadows of darkness wavered and thinned. Meggie took her

chance and shot forward on her knees, still holding the shield before her for protection. Unfortunately, the vacillation of the shadows was only momentary. They marshalled again, and now intensified their concentration on her mind.

"Despair of escaping, despair of moving, despair of living, and end your pain. Put down your shield, put down your shield, put down your shield, for you strive in vain. We are the shadows, we are the shadows, and you join the shadows, of Barrowbane."

They had found her weakness. Meggie could stand and fight heroically against hostility, but against a rhythmic chant — even a flawed and monotonous one like this — she had no powers of resistance. The shield became as heavy as a rock. Meggie drooped and sank with it to the ground. Her awareness of pain was ebbing away fast. Oblivion was near.

Chapter 25

THE RIVER OF LAMENTATION

"ALL blessings to you, Queen Olwen Underhill," Meggie sobbed, "wherever you may be." Her tone was a mixture of relief and regret. She was still stunned from the shock of her confrontation with the shadows, and could hardly believe she had escaped intact.

When the plate had hit the ground, the magical green essence of life that it contained had somehow taken root under the pressure of the darkness and had sprouted in a flash into lush creepers. They had twined round Meggie as they grew and pulled her half-senseless body along with them out of the last doorway of Barrowbane and down a cliff-face. Meggie had come safely to rest on a ledge but, by the time she had gathered strength enough to pull on the creepers and bring the plate tumbling down after her, they had already withered and shrivelled away to brittle paper.

The plate which had saved her life was lost to the shadows forever, its power spent. She had briefly seen all the beautiful images of the countryside that she had carved upon it flashing in front of her eyes before fading into extinction. Then she had sat in dazed sorrow at the loss of her gift from the Queen of the Sidhe of the Green Earth, for she had come to love that gift dearly.

* * *

Now, after she had rested and recovered a little, she began to take stock of her new surroundings. The ledge on which

139

she sat seemed to stretch forever to left and right like a gash on the cliff-face. Below it, a river coursed swiftly, and above it sheer rock stretched vertically upwards further than the eye could see. Meggie could just make out the black hole of the doorway of Barrowbane many yards above her. Without knowing it, she must have been very close to its edge when the shadows overcame her. If she had had her own way, and conquered them with the first flashing lights from the plate, she would have hurled herself from the tunnel straight into the fast-flowing river, and would have been carried off downstream to drown. It seemed that those who had sought to destroy her had actually saved her from that fate. The forces of ill will also had their part to play, then, in shaping the harmony of creation.

She pondered on this new twist in events for a while, but her head was still throbbing too much to learn anything from it. She was beginning to shiver with cold as well. It was time to be moving again.

As far as she could make out, the river bank on the far side was wide and flat, with no obvious hazards. She did not know yet whether it would be better to continue journeying in the same direction as the tunnel of Barrowbane, or to turn and follow the river's course, but, come what may, it seemed better to cross to the far bank first, in case the cliff-ledge crumbled or disappeared further on.

Gripping tightly with her hands, she carefully lowered her legs into the water to test the strength of the current. It surged and pulled hazardously under the surface, as if the river were in spate. It would be dangerous to try to swim cross-stream. Quickly, she pulled herself back up on to the ledge again. What now? Dark, sticky liquid from the river was clinging to her legs. She wiped some on to a finger and sniffed it with distaste. Blood!

She remembered tales the Old Woman had once told her of an underground river of blood. She had called it the River of Lamentation. Into it the sorrowing Earth Mother let fall, like tears, all the blood of her children spilled in vain. Streams of it flowed downwards from battlefields and scenes of carnage in every land. The many tributaries joined into one swift river and poured away into the bowels of the world in misery and shame, so that the earth's green surface might be cleansed after its violation. The horror was that this river had never once dried up. The Earth Mother could never finish grieving.

If this blood-flow before her was the Old Woman's River of Lamentation — or even one of its smallest tributaries — Meggie knew with certainty that she could not survive if she tried to swim across it. Even if the treacherous currents did not kill her, the curse on its waters surely would. Now she could neither stay where she was nor move safely to any of the four quarters, lest the water claim her. She belonged to it, and only to it could she appeal for help.

Reluctantly, she took the mother-of-pearl shell from her bag and put it to her lips. The haunting note reverberated again and again against the cliff-face, echoing and amplifying its arcane power. It seeped into her mind, her body and her soul. It beseeched her, entreated her, enticed her to come with the tides away, away to the sea, to dance in the waves and the deep, dark waters. She swayed on the edge, swimming in sound. The shell fell from her grasp into the swift flow and was lost. She could not stop following.

* * *

Although her soul was drowning, her body did not touch the river of blood and was saved. It was borne across the stream secretly by three blue maidens from the Isle of the Blessed. These three, who were unused to pain and sorrow, found the River of Lamentation too much to bear. Even in the short journey from one side to the other, they grew worn and weary, and passed away from life into the elemental water whence they came.

Upon the far shore Meggie lay still while her mind settled into a clear, mirrored pool. She felt empty and hollow as a dry reed in the wind, as if something inside her had died. Indeed it had. The three maidens of blue had been her empathy, her sympathy and her harmony.

Chapter 26

THE GREY PLAIN

THE horror of the river of blood seemed suddenly far behind her. Before her, the great plain of the future stretched like an endless opportunity. Although the terrain was unpromisingly flat and featureless, the sky dull and grey, its monotony was a welcome relief to her. At least there could not possibly be any hidden treachery in its open spaces. Moreover, it was lighter, and the atmosphere definitely less oppressive.

Forgetting the ache in her limbs, she walked tall and straight across the plain, with a spring in her step. The going was easy. She felt that she could cover many miles without tiring.

It was some while before she stopped again to reconnoitre, but she could not tell how long or how far she had come. Time and progress were impossible to gauge in the uniform greyness. Indeed, she asked herself as she turned now and surveyed the colourless flats around her on all sides, how could she know that she was going forward at all, and not just treading in pointless circles? There seemed to be nothing to aim for here, no goal to achieve.

With that realisation came disenchantment, and with disenchantment the further realisation that the grey plain, no less than the black tunnel and the blood river, also contained a hidden treachery. It neutralised her unique moods and tones, her creative character, and her self-asserting lust for a challenge. Its vastness diminished her humanity to the merest speck of nothing in the boundlessness of empty space. She had become a cipher in an infinite calculation, whose continuity was a law from which she could not escape. Her soul was lost.

The grey matter of endless opportunity now became the stuff of nightmare. She tried to break free from it, but the faster she ran the more insubstantial the ground became beneath her, until it could no longer support her weight. Her limbs slipped from under her, flailing and thrashing in nothing, getting nowhere. She gulped the air in desperation. It was thinning too. She was gasping for enough breath to cry for help, but the sound that issued from her parched throat just died in the emptiness. The rarified air could not carry it.

"Think!" she commanded herself. "Think before you die!" With difficulty she managed to focus her agitated mind back to the still pool it had been before she set out on her journey over the great plain. As she did so, its becalmed surface reflected back the grey blankness outside, suspending her in counterbalance with it. This did not get her any further forward, but it was a life-sustaining compromise. As she floated motionless in the indeterminate substance, expending no energy, she could at least breathe freely again. Once or twice she tried moving and calling, but to no avail. There was nowhere for body or sound to go, and the effort left her quite out of breath. It was energy wasted. She would have to try some other tack.

The apple branch would be useless, she thought at first. If the greyness completely muffled her own strong voice, the tiny tinkle of the Apple would stand no chance at all, unless . . . it was a long shot, but worth a try.

As calmly as she could, she drew the flowered twig from her bag and shook it gently. At first she could hear nothing, but then, ever so faintly, she felt its sound vibrating, with sweet notes like tiny bells and the first cries of new-born spring creatures. Then, instead of fading away quickly as it did on the surface of the earth, the resonance of the Apple song opened out and filled the virgin, empty space around her. The dull greyness began to sparkle like specks of dust

144

in a shaft of sunlight, and the faintest fragrance of apple blossom filtered through the air.

Meggie let herself relax completely in its soothing balm, her anguish over. Her hunch had been correct. Her own voice had been too dense and heavy for the rarified particles of grey to carry, but the delicate voice of the Apple — which was so fine that few people could hear it at all — was of just the right quality to set this subtle air a-dancing. It buoyed her spirits too, lifting her half-way to meet the Raven.

Beautiful Brigit, clothed in the sparkling plumage of the White Raven, hovered in the grey sky above her.

"Throw up the apple twig," she called. "Without it I do not have the power to carry you in this thin, dull atmosphere. I can take you as far as the Portal of the Northern Wind, but beyond that point I cannot pass, for I am a creature of Air and do not exist where no wind blows."

Meggie threw up the apple twig. It rose slowly, as if against some resistance, leaving a sparkling trail behind it through which Meggie could ascend. She landed softly on the Raven's back.

"Keep your thoughts light and your ideals high. Above all, don't look down, or your fear of falling will make your weight impossible to bear."

The Raven gave these last instructions hurriedly, before catching the floating apple twig in her beak.

Meggie kept her eyes tight shut as they giddily ascended, trying to keep her mind fixed on her pleasant memories of gliding in the apple scent above the Fair Plain of Ever-Dawn. In contrast, her present flying sensations were not agreeable at all. As they drove upwards, the unyielding grey air buffeted and battered her solidity, as if it would tear her into a million thin shreds. The White Raven had the worst of it. Meggie could feel her wing muscles distended and her neck stretched long and tight with the strain. She wished she could have spared her, but now that they had started, there was no going back.

145

Soon, there was no going forward either. The grey air above formed an invisible but impenetrable barrier. The Raven felt it first and pulled back her neck instantly in alarm, blowing the apple twig out of her beak like an arrow.

"Fare you well, Meggie, and true be your thought," she called, swooping downwards under her and away on the wind.

* * *

It all happened so quickly that Meggie did not even have time to fall. The apple dart hit the force field with a loud crack like thunder, and shattered into countless miniscule pieces like a cloud of dust. Then the whole world seemed to topple head over heels in reaction.

When the dust eventually settled, it must have formed a thin skin over the grey invisibility, because Meggie could now see what was really there. Her feet seemed to be back on solid ground again too. Behind her, the plain stretched out as monotonously and endlessly as before, but in front of her were two gates, high and wide as mountain ranges. They were guarded by a burly, bearded giant, so tall that the top of his head seemed to disappear into the sky.

"I am Boreas, keeper of the Northern Portal. Why come you here?" His voice boomed and roared like a winter gale. It was somewhat daunting, but not threatening. Meggie cleared her throat.

"To seek the Well at the World's End."

"And whom do you seek there?"

"She who is my true teacher, the one who bears the face of the Goddess for me."

"And do you wish to seek this one more than you wish to keep life itself?"

"I do," said Meggie, knowing that after travelling all this distance, and having risked her life so often already, it would be absurd to answer otherwise.

"Then pass, and may you find what you are seeking."

Chapter 27

THE CASTLE OF GLASS

THERE had been an ear-shattering, tearing sound, accompanied by an icy blast of wind. It had started at the top of the great gates as high as mountains and worked downwards, seemingly straight through the giant and the ground under Meggie's feet. As it went, the whole landscape appeared to split asunder as if it were a piece of screening material being ripped down the middle. Behind it was blackness.

It was not an oppressive, suffocating blackness like the tunnel of Barrowbane. It was simply empty, having nothing to give or take. Meggie stood passively within it, without thought or emotion, and waited.

At last, from the inky depths, one tiny point of light gleamed. Meggie noted it, but did not move in response. Soon another and then another appeared. Faster and faster they came now, until there were myriads of minute stars in clusters forming a white and shining track. Meggie could not tell whether it went up, down or straight ahead through the blackness, but it did not matter. She took one step and then another upon the track, until it took her into itself, and moved her effortlessly along.

She heard the many voices of the stars singing in harmony as they wheeled the vast and empty heavens. They sang in the universal language of creation: a language of colours, vowels and pure tones. They told her of a wise and ancient race that had once lived on the surface of the earth at the same place as she. They were taller and fairer than her own folk, more like unto the Sidhe with their auras of light. She heard these people sing songs of a Great Goddess beyond the gods and goddesses of earth, one whose name could not be uttered but whom they called Ioua, for that was the colour and sound of the stars as they sang her praises. Her body was the black vault of the night sky, and the stars within it were pulse points through which her quintessential power radiated across the cosmos.

That ancient race had been able to tune into stars. They knew that each star had its own tone through which an infinite source of energy could be tapped, and that each constellation of stars was a circuit of energy, like a vast memory of the forms of creation.

Meggie had a fleeting vision of these people, grouped upon the land in the pattern of a constellation, singing the pure notes of the component stars. Coded energy from them bounded and resounded across deep space to the green surface of the earth. It shimmered like a heat-haze in the air, enveloping the people in a column of silvery-white light. As the energy crystallised and was grounded, a conical hill rose up from nowhere, and thirteen tall black stones grew up around it, impressed with the maps of stars and containing their secret, vital power for all time.

The vision faded from sight and from mind, but it left Meggie with a calm, peaceful sense of strength, as if, for the first time, she knew deep inside who she really was. Then the white track of stars released her.

* * *

Before her, seven stars spun in concentric circles, with tails of light trailing behind them. They were like seven circular steps. As she climbed each one, it hummed with a note of the musical scale and a colour of the rainbow: seven notes and seven colours whose synthesis was the glittering, icy, fiery, black light of the Castle of Glass. It wheeled at the centre of the seven star-circles, silent and colourless, containing their seven-fold power.

Although Meggie had come to it openly, the Castle of Glass did not reflect that, or offer her sanctuary. Its icy, hard surface would only reflect a power that was sealed within. It would not unlock its gateways for any lesser force.

Meggie knew what she must do. Through the fathoms of her black, empty mind she probed until at last she found the Jewel of the Heart, pulsing with living light like the Sun. It was the hub of her being, just as the fearsome Castle of Glass was the hub of the universe on which the stars turned. She concentrated with all her power now upon the Jewel, feeding the furthest reaches of her mind into it, until it grew in size and strength and totally contained her. Within the Jewel, Meggie centred still on her own perfection, beaming light through rainbow facets in all directions. She burned with love.

Now the Castle, too, began to shine in its own true colours, until its walls were not of cold, icy, black glass, but of the same warm jewel-light as Meggie. She walked through its transparent gateway as liquid light through liquid light. There was no resistance. The words of Albina came to her: "This is the Jewel of the Heart, beyond price and beyond description. . . . By its power all things melt, and are won." Now she understood the nature of the Jewel's power. It did not conquer and subdue, but integrated and enlivened. It sought to enter things, not to invade and despoil, but to rejoice in their mysteries.

Then, in a flash of inspiration, Meggie knew that Albina had said "one" and not "won": by its power are all things one. For an ecstatic moment, Meggie experienced the full power of the circling heavens as her own, but instantly the feeling shattered with a high, piercing sound like a million splintering icicles, and she was flung with great force to the ground.

As she lay, dazed and disoriented, the Castle of Glass wheeled about her without a break in its icy, hard walls, but it had melted for her, and it was won.

Chapter 28

THE WASTELAND

THE inside of the Castle was surprisingly small, Meggie thought, as she sat where she had landed at its centre. It contained nothing but a bare, earthen floor. The turning circular walls were brilliant white from the inside, rather than black, but apart from that offered no new conditions. There seemed to be nowhere to go from here.

Then she moved, in the same direction as she had been flung. The walls moved out with her. The further she went, the more the walls receded and more bare earth floor appeared within them, but when she tried going back the way she had come, they closed in again. Going in any other direction seemed to make the floor tilt, so that she slid back as fast as she progressed. Always, she noted, she remained in the centre of the circle of the walls but it seemed that she could choose just how large that circle was to be. She decided then to keep to the first direction she had tried.

The walls began to roll back until they were but a dazzle of light on the far horizon, and the earthen floor expanded on all sides to meet it. It was a strange land indeed that she was creating as she walked, like a heather heath that had been blighted by some devastating pestilence. Its spiky thorn bushes and stunted trees were all as dead as stones and, indeed, the land was covered in stones of all shapes and sizes. They were poised at odd angles as if ready to take off at any moment and go about their business, but, apart from Meggie, nothing moved at all. There was not even a breath of wind to stir the sticks and stones into a semblance of activity.

With what few memories she had left to her, Meggie recalled the times she had gone with Gavin to observe the natural beauty around the glens. Even in the quietest spots there had never been a single moment of complete stillness such as this. A place without movement and change was unnatural, Meggie thought, without life or future. It was like the end of the world.

By and by, she came upon a circle of nine stone pillars. They looked like the Long Stones of home, but, unlike them, had no air of sacred vitality about them. She did not trust them, and passed them by. Shortly after, however, she realised that the light-walls of the Castle were beginning to close in on her, and the further she went towards them, the barer the earth became, till even stones were scarce. It did not feel right. She would have to go back. Again she tried to avoid the circle of pillars, but, whichever way she passed it, she noticed the distant walls start to advance, as if to urge her to enter, and eventually she conceded.

At the centre of the pillars a round, flat, slate-grey rock lay flush with the ground. She brushed it clear of stones and debris, and discovered a five-pointed star of perfect symmetry inscribed on its smooth surface. As she traced its never-ending lines with her finger, she felt its power, and knew it to be the blight that scathed the land. It was a source of pure hatred that allowed nothing to live or move within its domain, and that maintained the icy, eyeless walls of the Castle of Glass wheeling eternally round it like a prison, forbidding and foreboding.

Meggie felt grim. Now, stripped of all illusions, she knew what lay beyond the Northern Wind, beyond the point where anything that lived or loved could aid her. From the North the sun never shone, but winter sent its chilly sting to kill summer's gladness, and turn people cold and bitter as the frosty land. This stone before her was the scourge of life and joy, and as she looked on it her heart grew hard in judgement against it. Hard and cold grew her heart, slate-grey ice her eyes, immovable her being, until her enmity matched that of the stone itself. Her face now reflected the stone and the stone her face. Like mirrors, they flashed images of each other into eternity.

However, what Meggie saw on the stone she did not recognise as herself, for to her it was as cold and dark as the mask of Death. Many times on her journeys she and Death had given each other sidelong glances, and now, at the World's End, they met for the first time face to face. It was a hard confrontation.

"Love me," said Death.

"Never," retorted Meggie. "You kill my love, and all that it would nurture."

"That I do," admitted Death calmly, "but with my cold, killing winds comes the cloak of snow that protects the earth, and gives it rest from yielding. My snow is pure in colour and beautiful on the mountains. It contains life-giving water that strong shoots might spring anew. My touch is also kindly on the old and sick. Like a blessing, it releases them from their bodies of burden and pain, that their spirits can dance free and light as the sun in the sky. I am icy, stony Death, but I should not be denied. Love me."

"Never one time or again will I love you, Death. Even the unborn hope of love you have killed within me." Meggie had given up hope and innocent compassion long ago, it seemed, in order to reach this moment. It was a mockery to demand them of her again now.

"So be it, but you should know that that which I cut down is not lost, but after a season of rest returns transformed. And always its new form is greater and grander than the old could ever have been."

The words struck a chord. Meggie found herself replying automatically, as if it were the next line of a song that she was singing: "Is that always so?"

"Always," echoed Death, gently but sadly.

Meggie remembered. She herself had played the part of

Death, the grim Reaper, to sacrifice the Corn King. She herself had chosen to cut down Gavin, the one whom she had loved the best, so that in some mysterious way he could be transformed. To play the part of Death was a dismal responsibility, but to shirk it would put an end to the changes and movements that were essential to life. Death was so necessary, yet so misunderstood, and although his power was great, even he might be miserable without love. Now she replied:

"O dark and icy Death, even you have your place. Even you are part of the great harmony of the Mother of Creation, who ensouls all forms. In love she sends them freely forth from her, and in love she brings them back under her wing when their time comes. If I hated you, great, cold stone, it was because I denied that part of you that was in me. Now if I love you, perhaps you will feel the part of me that is surely in you — the part that lives, loves and moves."

Then she took the rock crystal from around her neck and kissed it.

"This jewel is a token of my love. The knots on its cord are nine like your pillars, and its golden arcs are as circular as you. We cannot be so different, then."

With a grin as impish as Gavin's, she tossed the crystal on to the stone. It landed at the very heart of the five-pointed star.

Chapter 29

THE WELL AT THE WORLD'S END

EVEN as rock hit rock, it changed. The mask of Death faded, and the smooth stone surface shimmered into a pool of crystal clear water. From each point of the silvery star, a river cascaded down through the land, bringing everything to life as it went. First the nine pillars sprouted into flourishing hazel trees, laden with ripe golden nuts. As the nuts fell, Meggie saw five salmon leap from the heart of the pool to catch them, then each one took to its own river, swam downstream and away.

Now the land was sparkling with activity as stones became plants, animals and birds. Small creatures scurried in the fresh green grasses. Bright butterflies fluttered upwards to the hum of bees. Everywhere flowers opened until the air was fragrant. Sheltering trees grew tall and proudly ruffled their leaves in the breezes. Most beautiful to Meggie's eyes were the blossoming apples, whose silvery-white petals flickered to the ground with a tinkle of tiny bells.

Golden horses now galloped through the meadow to greet her, whinnying in delight as they approached the hazel circle. She remembered them too, and patted them fondly as they nuzzled close. Then, with a toss of their silken manes they were away again, wild and unfettered as was their nature. She was happy to see these spirits of the corn, but happier still to let them go free, for now she shared their secret release from the fear of Death. She knew that Death did not lay waste unless he was denied his rightful power and purpose, for he and Love were but different masks of the force of evolution, which brings transformation into greater and grander forms. Between Death and Love life dances forever, and now she would dance with it.

Even as she began to move, a voice filled the air, warming her skin like sunlight. It was the voice of the Nameless One.

"This pool of the silvery star is the Well at the World's End. So deep is this Well, so deeply hidden in the heart among the interlaced roots of life itself, that it has never been brought to light since the ancient days when man walked naked in the sight of Sun and Moon, and hid himself not for shame. Since that time, man, in his deliberations, sealed off the deepest places within him until they moved no more, but turned to stone and ice, laying waste the fertile land of his imagination. Now nothing moves or melts the deepest heart of man to let the Well flow once more into the world.

"Even the mother who has lost her child, and weeps till she feels her very heart break, even she does not find the roots of this Well, for she weeps only for her beloved one, and not for the child of another who has fallen. Her love is not selfless, for it does not embrace the whole of creation. Though she feels her soul break into a thousand pieces, yea even still does this deeper Well remain unmoved, and devoid of life.

"Even the slave, bound and shackled, who gives his humanity to the fell Fates, that his soul might fly free when his flesh is broken on the wheel of cruelty — even he does not understand the mysteries of this Well. For insofar as his heart is pitted against his captors and torturers, insofar as his spirit stands proud against those who would break it, to that extent the deeps of this Well remain as stone and ice for him, and he sends the cold chill of death upon those who bind him.

"At this place — the Well of the hidden heart at the World's End — hate and love, death and life, cold stone and gentle waters: all opposites are reconciled. Each makes of them what they will by their actions and reactions. In the Foretime, all knew its secrets. Now but few can penetrate the depths as you have, and let that source flow.

"Many wonders have you seen upon your journeys, and many wonders are yet to come. But the wonders of this Well are the most profound. The nuts of the nine hazels are the kernels of wisdom. The salmon who eat of them are the five aspects of the soul. With the nuts of wisdom they swim down the streams of the five Arts, bringing seeds of inspiration and vision to the people of the world who drink at the streams when they dream. But you will drink of the Well itself, which is the source of all understanding. Its waters will consecrate you with light.

"But first you must finish your quest. You have come here to see the face of the one you seek in the waters of the Well. When you are ready, then, you may look, and see what you can see."

Meggie could not bring herself to look straight away. Her mind was still whirling with excitement at her discovery of the Well at the World's End. The way it had happened was more beautiful than her wildest dreams had imagined, and she was bubbling with happiness at her achievement. It was a feeling to be savoured, and not rushed. There was time a-plenty here to find the face of her teacher in the water. First she would dress the Well to prepare for the special moment.

She gathered armfuls of apple-blossom and strewed them in coiling patterns between the five streams round the pool. Then she dug up tiny plants and transplanted them carefully into the spaces, so that they made pictures of the marvels she had seen and heard on her journeys. The nine hazels leaned their branches low to learn from these new images, and the wisdom they gained they stored in the golden nuts. Again the salmon leapt from the pool to catch the kernels, and again they swam downstream to bring these visions into the world.

Meggie worked long and hard until the garden of the Well

was even more lovely than Nature had intended, and that was no mean task. At last she was ready. She picked five-petalled Moon-white roses from the hedges, their centres as golden as the Sun, and set them floating like boats on the pool. Then she took in a deep breath of the perfumed air.

Long and slow she let out the breath, relaxing all anticipation, and melting into the moment. Long ago, the Old Woman had taught her to let go like that, and Gavin had shown her why. She would not spoil this special event by trying too hard to see. As she breathed out, the water gently rippled. When the surface came smooth again, she knew that the hidden face of the Goddess would be revealed.

* * *

Now, although time in that place does not stand still as it does in the formless realms of eternity, it does not move with a regular beat either. Sometimes many suns and moons can cross its path without an hour passing on the surface of the earth, but, at other times, the shortest moment can last for years by the world's reckoning.

Such a moment was Meggie's breath upon the pool, that sent ripples down the five streams. How long, you ask, can a breath last? If it means as much to the breather as that one did to Meggie, if it is so full of import and intent as that one was, it can last for a whole aeon — a great age of creation. And so it did.

While Meggie sat upon the edge of the Well at the World's End, waiting for the answer to her final quest, many things changed in the land that she came from. As the generations came and went in the clachan, many of the ancient traditions were lost, until at last the Circle was but a memory in the minds of the old. They talked, too, of the legendary Apple Tree whose fruit ripened the whole year long and whose branches sang, but with the passing of the old ways its magic must have faded, for now there was no

157

such tree. The young stopped believing in it. The blackest day came when the Long Stones were broken up, so that their field could be ploughed and walls built from the rubble. Soon after that the crops failed, and disease struck. Within a generation there was no one left to tend the land. The heather thatch fell in on the old stone cottages and only sheep roamed the glens.

Now that might have been the end of the story. Meggie's land, like so many to the south, might have lost its green face completely under concrete. Industrial pollution and city squalor might have proved so inhospitable that the Sidhe — who maintain the delicate balance of Nature's creations on which we all depend — might well have abandoned the land to its fate, as they have elsewhere. But that was not to be.

The five streams from the Well that Meggie had allowed to flow, the hazelnuts of her inspiration that the salmon of wisdom bore to dreamers, and the ripples of her calm breath upon the water of the pool, maintained between them a mystical bond between man and the land of Scotland. No matter what befell through ignorance or greed, the mists of the Sidhe still swirled through the glens and wove their magic, so that Nature was not ravaged and the wisdom of the past never quite obliterated. Throughout the centuries many could still feel the heartbeat of the Earth and the pull of the Moon. Some even heard the stars sing, for the rocks of the Long Stones that were scattered across the land still somehow managed to survive and relay their secrets. Some found the doorways that Meggie had opened, and entered the realms of the Sidhe for themselves. Of these, some returned to tell their tales, but others again did not.

Even on the surface of the earth, artists and mystics of all kinds always found inspiration in the fey and dreamy beauty of the Scottish landscape. The images that Meggie grew in the garden of the Well were woven by the Sidhe into wonderful visions that shone through the forms of nature.

Again and again they appeared in legend, song, craft and art. Their power to entrance never really died.

When Meggie went on her journey beyond the Northern Wind, the Scottish capital of Edinburgh was but a fortified village overshadowed by its volcanic hills. Over the centuries it grew in size and importance, but perhaps the waters of the Well affected it too, for it never did turn, like other capitals, into an ugly sprawling metropolis bereft of green. Many favourite haunts of the Sidhe still grow wild and free within the very heart of the city, and it is famous as a patron of the many arts, rather than of heavy industry.

Part Six

Full Circle

Chapter 30

JANEY

W HEN her father had announced that they were going to move to Edinburgh, Janey had been horrified. Her mother talked on enthusiastically about opportunities for education and how much more money they would have, and her sister Fiona, who was at the age when village life was quite boring, immediately fell in love with the idea.

Janey, as usual, was the odd one out. Her mind reeled at the thought of leaving the west coast village where she had been born and brought up. She belonged here. To go away, especially to a city, would just break her heart. She could not understand how the others were prepared to leave without even a qualm. There was nothing she could do about it, though. Her father had already accepted a new post, and bought a house there. She would just have to go along with the rest of the family and learn to live with it.

The day before they left was particularly bleak. Her parents were fussing over the removals, and her sister had gone out with friends to celebrate. Janey was moping about the house — getting in the way, her mother said — so after lunch she decided to make herself scarce.

She walked round the glens behind the village for the last time, retracing old steps and reliving memories. The glens were both her friend and her home. She always came to them alone, and told them her feelings as she went round, sure that they understood and responded. Today she said nothing, but the black clouds scudding shadows across her path echoed her thoughts nevertheless, and the empty,

163

roofless walls of abandoned cottages knew what she was going through.

She climbed the little hill at the head of the glens and looked down past the sheep slopes, boulders and burns, to the red pantiled roofs of the new houses at the edge of the village. Behind them, sea stretched out to sky.

"Some day," she said aloud now to the landscape, "when I'm old enough to make my own decisions, I'm going to come back here to live, and then I'm not going to leave again — ever."

Old Ben, one of the retired fishermen who sat on the waterfront mending nets that would never be used again, had once told her that promises or wishes made on this hill always came true. He had said it in a mock-serious tone as if he were pulling her leg, but Janey preferred to believe that he had really meant it.

* * *

At first she had tried to make an effort to settle in to please her parents. She had gone with her mother for morning coffee to Princes Street on Saturdays, and with Fiona to parties and discos with her new school friends. But Princes Street to her was a limbo of endless faces with no life or purpose about them, and parties made her feel like a fish out of water. She could never think of anything to say to the people she met, and would end up sitting by herself looking miserable. Dumb insolence her mother called it, but she was not trying to be unfriendly. It was just that she did not fit in. How could you explain to city folk that you were more lonely in their company than you were on your own on a hilltop or by the evening seashore? No one would know what you were talking about.

It took about a year before she came to accept Edinburgh on her own terms. She had got a puppy for Christmas, and with it had discovered many wild, natural places around the city where she could feel free again. Now she spent her weekends walking with the dog, familiarising herself with the rugged beauty of her new stamping-grounds.

Sometimes she went to Silverknowes beach, where at low tide the receding sea left silvery curving fingers on the rippled grey sand, and Fife, across the water, looked swathed in mists like another world out of time. From there she might walk up-river, through the evocative aroma of wild garlic and dank moss, to Cramond's Old Mill, where you could sit on the railing overlooking the waterfall. She would watch the perpetual motion of the smooth sheet of water rushing, hissing and dashing, spraying diamonds against the rocks, until its movement hypnotised her into feeling that she was flowing and falling down along with it.

She loved watching the living sculpture of the water, but the dog remained unimpressed. He preferred Corstorphine Hill, with its interesting woods, and — if the wind was in the right direction — the exotic cries of the animals in the zoo on the other side. Or, on hot days, what could be better than a paddle in the shady burn at the Hermitage of Braid?

There were many places that Janey found in Edinburgh where the pulse of nature was still louder than that of civilisation, but perhaps her favourite was the volcanic hill of Arthur's Seat. She could see it from her bedroom window and, in the mornings when it was skirted in low-lying haar from the sea, she could imagine that it was not part of the city at all, but a piece of her own glens that she had brought with her.

During the holidays she had climbed it almost daily, till now she knew its every curve and contour, rubbled landslide and craggy face. She knew which paths led to the top, and which petered away precariously to nothing on steep slopes. She knew the sheltered, grassy valleys, and the bare, exposed fronts where wind blew you flat against sharp whins. She knew the ancient terraces, the Wells and the ruined Chapel.

She also knew the Lochs. Dunsapie, always in shadow, seemed cold and foreboding. Duddingston had guardian geese who would give you a really nasty peck from behind if you made yourself at home. St Margaret's was the best, she decided. Oblivious to clouds of midges, she would sit on its banks for hours while the dog sniffed out rabbits on the hill behind her. She would follow the track of a single duck or seagull across the water, until she got lost in the ripples as birds bobbed and landed, and took off in her imagination to the syncopated rhythms of their calls.

She knew that in times gone by lochs, wells and springs had been considered sacred, and each had had its own guardian nymph or goddess. She liked to fancy that this loch had a guardian too, named Margaret of course, though not the historical queen and Christian saint, but a pagan spirit of healing and magic. In offering to Margaret of the Loch, Janey brought bread for the ducks whenever she came, and usually threw a wishing-stone into the water for good luck too.

She never told anyone about her adventures on the hills, or about Margaret of the Loch. It was her own private world, made real by secrecy, that she could enter when alone.

Chapter 31

HALLOWE'EN JOURNEYS

THE day had started badly. Janey was having a long lie reading, and dreaming about Hallowe'en. She was lost in a ballad about her namesake, making up tunes to the verses, and acting out the story in her mind.

> Janet has kilted her green kirtle
> A little abune her knee,
> And she has braided her yellow hair
> A little abune her bree.
>
> She prinkd hersell and prinnd hersell,
> By the ae light of the moon,
> And she's away to Carterhaugh,
> To speak wi young Tamlane.
>
> She hadna pu'd a double rose,
> A rose but only twae,
> When up and started young Tamlane,
> Says, 'Lady, thou pu's nae mae.
>
> 'When I was a boy just turnd of nine,
> My uncle sent for me,
> To hunt and hawk, and ride with him,
> And keep him companie.
>
> 'There came a wind out of the north,
> A sharp wind and a snell,

And a deep sleep came over me,
And frae my horse I fell.

'The Queen of Fairies keppit me
In yon green hill to dwell,
And I'm a fairy, lyth and limb,
Fair Ladye, view me well.

'This night is Halloween, Janet,
The morn is Hallowday,
And gin ye dare your true love win,
Ye hae nae time to stay.

'The night it is good Halloween,
When fairy folk will ride,
And they that wad their true love win,
At Miles Cross they maun bide.'

Gloomy, gloomy was the night,
And eiry was the way,
As fair Janet, in her green mantle,
To Miles Cross she did gae.

Suddenly, right across fairyland, Fiona burst in.

And first gaed by the black, black steed,
And then gaed by the brown;
But fast she gript the milk-white steed,
And pu'd the rider down.

"Janey, I've just had this great idea! Why don't we have a
Hallowe'en party? Dad says we can use the garage. If we
start now, we can get it all decorated by this evening. I know
where we can get some really creepy masks!"

Janey was still at Miles Cross.

They turned him in her arms an eagle,
And then into an ass;
But she held him fast, and feared him not,
The man that she loved best.

She took a long time to reply.

"No thanks. That is, it doesn't seem right. Hallowe'en is, well, a time to be quiet . . . to *feel* things . . . not to blare disco music to kingdom come. . . ."

They turned him into a flash of fire,
And then a naked man;
She wrapt him in her green mantle,
And sae her true love wan.

"Don't be so stupid! You're just trying to put the dampers on 'cause it's my idea, aren't you? But you don't really mean it. Please come and help."

Up then and spake the Queen of Fairies,
Out o a bush o broom . . .

"I just can't. I really don't want a party. Can't really explain . . ."

'Had I but kennd, Tamlane,' she says,
'Before ye came frae hame,
I wad taen out your heart o flesh,
Put in a heart o stane.'

Fiona did not wait for an explanation. She just stalked out of the room and slammed the door behind her. The atmosphere of Tamlane was well and truly shattered now.

Janey got dressed and crept about the house, trying to keep out of Fiona's way. She could sense that her sister was in a really black mood. They managed to avoid each other until lunchtime, when their mother called them both into the kitchen to help with the food. Janey tried to keep quiet, to give the semblance, at least, of a truce, but Fiona was out to win her point. She kept digging with sarcastic comments, bringing up all the old unresolved arguments she could think of, in an attempt to provoke Janey into response. She could not stand her sister's introverted silences.

Their mother tried to intervene eventually, and Fiona blew up at her too. That was the limit. Janey grabbed her walking-jacket from the door, stuffed an apple in each pocket in lieu of lunch, and left the charged atmosphere of the house behind her.

Walking down the road, she could still hear them shouting. The dog had joined in too, howling with disappointment because Janey had not taken him with her. If she felt any pang of regret at walking out like that, it was for leaving the dog behind, but, otherwise, it was the right thing to have done. The cool air outside calmed her deeply.

She went to Arthur's Seat, choosing a route to the left of the main hill, along the top edge of Salisbury Crags. The place was deserted — strangely so for a Saturday afternoon — as if the spirit of Hallowe'en was keeping the world at bay. She made her way slowly along the length of the ridge, the sea-winds blustering round her face. To her left, the Crags fell steeply away, and beyond them lay the jumbled, busy roof-scape of the Old Town and University. To her right, the hill rolled down into an enclosed, grassy valley, already shadowy and subdued with dusk.

It was like walking on a crack between worlds: the great gulf on the one hand to the bustle of a twentieth-century city, and the timeless capsule of Nature gently breathing on the other. She had walked that crack her whole life, she thought to herself.

At the far end of the Crags she turned down the slope. St Margaret's Loch was a flat, grey mirror of the sky far below her. No birds ruffled its surface now.

On an impulse, she climbed to the bottom of a little gully halfway down the hillside. In the summer she had discovered that it entirely blotted out the interminable rumble of the city traffic, so she had spent a lot of time there, pretending she was far from civilisation. Now she did not have to pretend. The silence in the gully was so tangible she could almost touch it. It made her feel as alert and aware as an animal. Her first impulse was to turn and run, but she made herself stay. Her own words echoed through her head: "Hallowe'en is a time to be quiet . . . to *feel* things." She owed it to herself to try.

She sat on a stone in the grey silence, but after a while she had to admit that all that she felt was damp, cold limbs and numb feet. She also felt a little shamefaced at the argument with her sister. Perhaps it was time to swallow her pride and go back home to the party.

First she ate the two apples, throwing the cores away into a corner. She got up then, but she never did leave.

* * *

All things must come to an end. The ripples on the water died away, and its calm surface shimmered clear as a mirror. At last Meggie saw the face that she had been journeying for and waiting for, for so long.

She had learned through experience always to expect the unexpected, but, even so, the sight of that face really took her aback. It was her own, and its expression was not at all pretty. What could this mean? Even at the World's End was she to remain mocked and fooled?

Stunned and shaking, she splashed water from the Well on to her face, and gulped it down without thinking into her dry mouth. Then, of course, she saw the light.

She suddenly pealed with laughter, sending flocks of tiny birds twittering into the air from the hazels as if they were sharing the joke. For now she understood the oath she had made to the Sidhe, which had bound her to this curious quest. "I would give my life if I could", she had said, and so she had. She had bequeathed her mortality to the land she loved.

The four Elements of Earth, Air, Fire and Water were nothing less than the stuff of life out of which all the forms of Nature were spun and woven by the faery spirits. Meggie had given her own share of these Elements, in the form of the four tokens, back to the Sidhe to do with what they would, in order to complete her final journey. She had nothing of them left for herself.

The Castle of Glass, turning endlessly in the hidden centre of deep space, was the eternal Wheel of Death and Rebirth. Meggie had broken it, penetrated its secrets, and it could hold no more sway over her. Evermore she would abide in the fifth Element, which is the soul that breathes life into the myriad forms of Nature from the heart of the Nameless One.

Now, as she looked once more upon her face in the water, Meggie could see that there was no part of her that was not of the Great Goddess. She bore one of the countless names and faces of the Nameless One. She thought of the many others that she knew. There was Brigit, the maiden midwife; Cerridwen who tends the Magic Cauldron of Inspiration; Gwynhyfar, the White Moon-Queen; Morgana of the Dark Waters of Enchantment; Annis, her own guiding light, and so many more.

Had they all once been like her, she wondered: simple people who, by the unfathomable turns of Fate, had found the Heart of the Great Mystery and were clothed in the essence of eternity? And was she now like them: charged never to return to the surface of the earth except in timeless moments when people lifted up their hearts and minds in greeting, through the ancient rituals and in the hallowed places of the land? Would she, like the other identities of the Nameless One, live on in the cycles of myth, story and song that are passed down the generations, forgotten sometimes only to resurge later like flowers in springtime? Would people sing of her at the fireside on cold, winter nights, and welcome her into the homes and hearths of their imaginations? Would they appeal to her when they needed love and understanding?

Meggie realised now that she belonged not to one family or one glen, but to all the hidden children of the Goddess on the surface of the earth, through all the ages to come. She had gone beyond the limitations of life and death to become her own teacher, and her own reflection. It was the most beautiful and most sorrowful realisation of her whole existence.

With a mixture of joy and grief, contentment and dismay, she fell to weeping, weeping without ceasing until her soul flowed out in tears through the Blessed Well and the five sacred streams that revitalise the land. She wept until she thought that she could never rise again, for she felt the burden of all creation on her shoulders: the birth-pangs of the Earth when the first mountains were heaved up from its liquid fire, the death agonies of great stars that had exploded aeons before the Earth had ever been, and the chaos of old universes imploding to form other worlds where life could evolve anew.

All around her, the garden of the Well grew new pictures for the hazels, and the salmon leapt to catch the nourishing nuts of their wisdom for the world. Meggie's tears hung over the land that day like an invisible web of power. Many strange changes came over people as their dreams, or their nightmares, surfaced into their waking reality.

At last, she heard the Primal Word — the secret name of the Nameless One that is the first sound of creation. There was no part of her that was not of the Great Goddess. There were no more quests or questions, no more tokens or teachers, no more striving or misunderstanding. All was peace.

Oh so weary, she curled into a small ball by the water's edge and slept like a new-born child, and the Well, to which she had given so much, flooded its banks to contain her. Then its waters began to spiral upwards into a sixth stream, like a column of light.

Up through the light Meggie twirled like a feather, empty and unbound, her oath fulfilled. The light was silvery like water, sparkling and tingling fizzily inside her. Then it was the heather-purple of the hill-slopes of home, glorious and noble. Then it became a soft apple-green, so delicately scented. How she kissed and caressed that green! How it made her dance and sing! She felt like a tender new leaf breaking through treebark, unfolding, unfurling, and surging with sap. This was living!

* * *

The corner by the apple cores began to glimmer with light. Janey felt her heart thumping wildly, but she was not frightened, more excited. The light whirled silvery, purple and then green, settling into a radiant oval as tall as the gully itself. At its centre was a human form, brightly shining. Even as Janey watched, the light contracted and condensed, so that the inner being took on dimension and solidity.

It was a young woman. She was dressed in a flowing silken robe, gathered into a coiling, golden belt. Her green cloak, embroidered with cornstalks, flowers, crescent moons and star-spirals, was clasped at the throat with a silver brooch, in the form of a five-pointed star surrounded by nine amethysts. Red ribbons were braided through her long, black hair. She smelled of summer in the glens.

Janey realised that she was staring with her mouth open.

"Hello, who are you?" she asked, just to break the silence. It sounded totally stupid and inadequate — not to mention rude — but it was the best she could think of on the spur of the moment.

174

Meggie tinkled in merry giggles at this fine question. Who was she indeed? She was a facet of the Great Goddess, a creature of myth and magic, a free spirit who metamorphosed with the cycles of the seasons and climates of belief. She was also herself. She answered in the only way she could.

"Through the long ages I have been known by many names, but you may call me Meggie."

Janey's eyes came alight and alive with hope and wonder. Meggie could see the girl's bright soul dancing in delight within them.

"Then you must be . . . are you really my Margaret . . . my Margaret of the loch?"

Meggie only smiled. She could have told the girl that she both was and was not. She could have told her that the vision of your heart's desire is not a single fixed thing that you see once, but is ever-evolving as your understanding of it deepens. These things and many more could she have told her, but there was no need. The little one would realise for herself whatever she had to, when the time was right. Instead, Meggie held out her hand and said simply: "Come."

Hand in hand with her faery queen, Janey climbed out of the little gully on to the hillside. Through the swirling twilight mists in front of her she could see a squat heather-thatched cottage where nothing had been before. Beside it was the most magnificent Apple Tree, just covered in silvery-white blossoms.